There Was No Need to Tell Him in Words

Her mind toyed with the image of an ice cube submerged in hot water. She pictured the way such an ice cube shatters from the inside, splintering as it expands against itself. That was how she felt now, externally unchanged but completely altered from within, her soul sparkling like a jewel with countless facets of light.

He had asked her to trust him, and then he reached beyond her surface of ice to transform her.

D0048674

Dear Reader:

SILHOUETTE DESIRE is an exciting new line of contemporary romances from Silhouette Books. During the past year, many Silhouette readers have written in telling us what other types of stories they'd like to read from Silhouette, and we've kept these comments and suggestions in mind in developing SILHOUETTE DESIRE.

DESIREs feature all of the elements you like to see in a romance, plus a more sensual, provocative story. So if you want to experience all the excitement, passion and joy of falling in love, then SILHOUETTE DESIRE is for you.

Karen Solem
Editor-in-Chief
Silhouette Books

ARIEL BERK
Breaking the Ice

Silhouette Desire

Published by Silhouette Books New York

America's Publisher of Contemporary Romance

SILHOUETTE BOOKS
300 E. 42nd St., New York, N.Y. 10017

Copyright © 1985 by Barbara Keiler

Distributed by Pocket Books

ISBN: 0-373-05216-2

First Silhouette Books printing June, 1985

10 9 8 7 6 5 4 3 2 1

America's Publisher of Contemporary Romance

Printed in the U.S.A.

ARIEL BERK

is not only a novelist, she is a composer. In her spare time she enjoys activities as disparate as sailing, sunbathing, hiking, and visiting museums, but she lets nothing take too much time away from her pleasure in writing.

Silhouette Books by Ariel Berk

Silent Beginnings (DES #93)
Promise of Love (DES #154)
Remedies of the Heart (DES #180)
Hungry for Love (DES #194)
Breaking the Ice (DES #216)

1

It happened fast, so fast that only Emily's reflexes, and those of the driver in front of her, saved them both from disaster. The road running south from Litchfield rarely had heavy traffic, even now, during the evening rush hour; nobody, thank heavens, was driving in the opposite direction. The car cruising in the southbound lane ahead of Emily was a gleaming black BMW, obviously fairly new. The driver abided by the speed limit, which made Emily suspect that he wasn't from the area. Most locals in the sparsely populated Litchfield Hills ignored the speed limits on the lightly traveled country routes that connected one town with the next.

The driver's-side window of Emily's dilapidated station wagon was open, admitting the mild June breeze into the car. It tugged at the loose ends of the ponytail that she'd put her strawberry-blond hair in for work. She settled back in the driver's seat, enjoying the lush greenery on either side of the road—farm acreage to

her left, dense forest beyond a narrow swath of un-
mowed grass to her right. Soon the region would be
jammed with summer tourists. She appreciated the
relative emptiness of the road, her attention more on
the picturesque scenery than on the black BMW in front
of her.

Then, suddenly, a deer appeared, a graceful arc of
tawny brown energy galloping out of the forest toward
the asphalt. A yearling, Emily instinctively estimated by
its size. It cantered directly to the BMW, which veered
sharply across the double yellow line into the vacant
northbound lane, but a collision was unavoidable. The
deer glanced off the car's front fender, then stumbled
away and stared directly at Emily, its eyes uncannily
resembling hers, large and dark and glassy with terror.

She jammed her foot on the brake and her tires
locked, putting her car into a minor skid. She barely
missed the rear bumper of the BMW, which had
swerved back into her lane and then off the road,
coasting to a halt on the shoulder. Emitting a panicked
gasp, Emily released the brake, and the station wagon
rolled to a stop on the shoulder behind the black car.

She gripped the steering wheel to still her trembling
fingers and waited until she was able to breathe again,
until she was no longer deafened by the hectic drumming of the pulse in her temples. Taking a long breath,
she glanced toward the grass. The deer was gone.

With another deep breath, she reached for her door
handle and swung the door open. The driver of the
BMW had already emerged from his car and was
jogging around the front of it to check his fender. Emily
closed her door and studied him.

He was tall, nearly half a foot taller than her five feet
eight inches, and his physique was lean. He wore new
blue jeans and a pale blue oxford shirt with its sleeves
rolled up to his elbows. His head was crowned with

thick black curls. She was unable to see his face as he moved around his car and bent down.

Her hands were still shaking, and she rubbed her damp palms along her thighs, letting the faded denim of her well-worn dungarees absorb the moisture. She turned to the woods, searching for the deer, but didn't spot him.

The man was squatting by his car's right front fender, and Emily heard a muffled curse drift back to her on the warm late spring wind. She approached him hesitantly, remaining at the rear of his car as he hunkered down next to the tire to examine the damage. "Are you all right?" she called to him.

He turned to her, and his shocking eyes seemed to paralyze her momentarily. They were blue, an incredibly light blue, as hard and cold as ice. Given his black hair, the matching black mustache framing his upper lip, and his bronze complexion, she wouldn't have expected him to have such pale eyes.

They riveted her feet to the gravelly shoulder, and she struggled against their unnerving brilliance as he slowly stood. She was vaguely aware that he was remarkably handsome, his brow high, his nose long and straight, his jaw a stubborn angle. His build was exceptional, Emily admitted, feeling an unwanted blush heat her round, freckled cheeks.

He was assessing her, too, she realized as his stunning eyes ran over her with precision, taking in her messy reddish-blond ponytail and her heart-shaped face with its uptilted nose, soft pink lips, and dusting of girlish freckles, then moving down her body, clad in a striped T-shirt and aged jeans, and finally lifting again to her large, doelike eyes.

She felt fat. She wasn't, but the dictates of fashion and the changing taste of her ex-husband rendered her occasionally self-conscious about her somewhat robust, curvaceous body. Her weight fell comfortably within the range the insurance charts listed for her height, but Emily was convinced that those charts were composed not by doctors but by big, hearty midwestern women like her mother, who maintained that the nourishment of starving waifs in India was directly dependent on whether or not Emily finished her peas.

By now, nearly two years after her divorce, she rarely succumbed to self-consciousness about her broad shoulders, her solid, oval calves, her sturdy hips and full breasts. But something about the steely gaze of the man before her seemed critical, and she winced inwardly and irrationally vowed to go on a diet.

"I'm all right," he said, reminding Emily that she'd asked him a question. It seemed as if a year had passed since his eyes had fastened on her and frozen her. His voice was soft, a muted baritone. "How are you?"

Her tongue seemed strangely inflexible, so she answered with a nod. Turning to survey the woods, she felt her muscles unclench as she searched the shadows for the deer. "Do you see him?"

The man muttered something under his breath, and then bent down by his car again. "He nailed my fender."

"You nailed him," Emily remarked in the deer's defense.

"The hell with that. Look what he did to my car!"

A completely unreasonable anger shot through Emily. Of course the man hadn't been at fault—he'd done the best he could to avoid hitting the deer. But she couldn't keep herself from leaping to the creature's defense. "Your car won't bleed to death," she snapped. "Who knows about that poor yearling?" Without a moment's thought, she started across the high grass in search of the injured animal.

At the edge of the woods she paused, not wanting to scare the deer with an abrupt motion. As if he wasn't already scared. If he was seriously injured, she knew he wouldn't be able to travel far from the road. Just far enough to hide himself, she figured. Her eyes carefully combed the undergrowth, and she risked a step into the forest's darkness. A chipmunk responded to her movement, scampering up the thick trunk of an oak tree and out of sight in the canopy of leaves above her head. She waited until the forest grew still again, then hazarded another step.

"Forget him," the man called to her. "He's all right."

Emily grimaced as the forest's denizens reacted to the intrusion of the man's voice. Branches shook as squirrels scampered for cover, and several birds broke free of their leafy camouflage and soared high into the clear early evening sky. She skimmed the woods, hoping that the deer might also react by showing himself, but he was well hidden.

Exhaling, she turned to discover the man standing several yards away, his feet concealed by the weeds and tall grass bordering the forest. She drifted into the clearing, glancing over her shoulder several times to see if she could catch the deer in motion. Frustrated by her inability to find the wounded animal, she planted her hands on her hips and glowered at the man, refusing to let his bizarre silver-blue eyes disconcert her. "What makes you so sure he's all right? You hit him pretty hard."

"He hit me pretty hard," the man remarked, his voice still soft, though he was clearly angry. "If he was hurt, he wouldn't have gone prancing back into the woods."

"No, but he might have gone limping back into the woods," she argued. "It's likely he'd try to hide himself."

"Then that's his business," the man declared. "Forget about him."

Emily couldn't. It was more than just her job to care

about animals; it was a part of her emotional makeup. She generally didn't work with wild animals, but that didn't make her worry any less about the deer's well-being. He might merely have been dazed and shaken by his collision with the man's car, or he might have been seriously injured. Cracked or broken bones, perhaps, or internal damage. He could be suffering terribly, and that possibility caused Emily to suffer in sympathy for the unfortunate animal.

She took a stride back toward the woods, searching. "Give up," the man growled. "He's gone."

"What makes you so sure?" she retorted.

The man opened his mouth to reply, then pressed his lips together and gave Emily a long, quizzical appraisal. He shrugged and turned to the road, evidently expecting her to follow. "It doesn't make any difference," he commented. "There isn't a whole hell of a lot you can do for him anyway."

"Says you," she sniffed, remaining by the forest's edge.

The man paused and pivoted back to Emily. He seemed irritated. Upset about the dent in his car's fender? she wondered. Or upset about her? "If he isn't hurt badly," he pointed out, "he'll take care of himself. If he is, you aren't going to be able to do anything about it."

"I might be able to," she disputed the man. "And if I can't . . . if I can't, the least I can do is put him out of his misery."

Something hard and bright flashed in the man's eyes. "Put him out of his misery?" he repeated bitterly. "Kill him, you mean?"

Naturally that wasn't what Emily wanted to do, but it would be kinder than to let the deer suffer a long, agonizing death. "I mean," she answered slowly, "put him out of his misery. If he's beyond hope, why leave him here to suffer?"

"Kill him, then," the man shot back, his voice brutally soft. "Go find him and kill him. Just don't be hypocritical about it."

"Hypocritical?" she echoed in surprise.

"If you want to kill him, just say so. Don't use pretty little phrases to disguise what you're doing. 'Put him out of his misery,'" he scoffed. "'Euthanasia.' 'Mercy killing.' If you want to kill him, be my guest, but don't dress it up in fancy language."

She stared at the man, her mouth agape, as she tried to make sense of his barely contained fury. "I *don't* want to kill him," she insisted. "I just don't want him to suffer, for heaven's sake. Maybe you're upset about your car getting dinged, mister, but don't take it out on me."

The man's gaze softened slightly, curiosity coloring the expression in his eyes. "What are you, a park ranger or something?" he asked, glancing at her outfit, which clearly wasn't a ranger's uniform.

"I'm a vet," Emily replied, somewhat placated by his gentler tone. At his bemused look, she elaborated, "A veterinarian."

His gaze swept over her one more time, weighing this new information. Although Emily didn't see him take a step toward her, he seemed somehow closer to her as he scrutinized her. "Is that what veterinarians do?" he asked quietly. "Kill animals?"

"What veterinarians do," she answered, matching his low tone, "is put animals out of their misery, preferably by treating and healing them. Sometimes that isn't possible." She twisted back to face the woods. "Are you going to help me look for the deer or aren't you?"

He waited a long moment before joining her at the

edge of the forest. They paced the line of trees in opposite directions, scanning the shadows. "This is ridiculous," the man finally shouted to Emily as he started back toward her. "We aren't going to find him."

She knew he was right. If the deer was severely afflicted, he wouldn't have been able to get far. He must be all right, she consoled herself. Stunned and bruised, maybe, but nothing more serious than that. Reluctantly she approached the man, and they plodded through the grass back to their cars.

She noticed the slight indentation in the chassis in front of his BMW's tire. "That's not so bad," she told him. "A few bangs with a hammer ought to straighten it out."

He studied the dent grimly, then twisted to look at her. "You're really a vet?" he asked.

His surprise at her occupation amused her, and she felt her lips spreading in a smile. "Why shouldn't I be one?" she challenged him.

"You look . . ." His eyes combed her again. "You look more like a college kid."

"I was a college kid, once," she said with a shrug. Her informal outfit was practical in her line of work, though she usually wore a white coat over her clothing to reassure her clients. The coat made her appear more like a medical practitioner to pet owners, and that seemed to matter to them. Their pets—her patients—didn't much care what she looked like. They'd as happily slobber over a pair of jeans as over an expensive dress.

"Look, I'm sorry if I was short with you," he apologized. The halting quality of his voice indicated to Emily that apologizing wasn't something he did with frequency.

She forgave him with another bright smile. "Hitting a deer isn't much fun. You're allowed to lose your temper."

"Can I—" He stopped himself, engaged in a silent mental debate though his eyes never left Emily. "Can I buy you a drink or something?"

His invitation seemed halfhearted to Emily, and as attractive as she found the man, she thought it best to refuse. "No, thanks. I've had a long day." She started back to her station wagon.

He caught her by the shoulder, holding her in place. His grip was firm; she felt the warm pressure of his fingers against her skin beneath the thin cotton of her shirt, and a shiver rippled through her flesh, ending somewhere between her hips. She was astounded by her body's unexpected reaction, and she kept her face averted, certain that she was blushing again.

"Are you married?" he asked.

The bluntness of his question brought a giddy laugh to her lips. "No," she answered. "Are you?"

"No." His hand tightened slightly on her shoulder, then relaxed as he eased her around to face him. "My name is Lloyd Gordon. I'm here for the weekend and I'd enjoy your company for dinner. That's all, just a drink and dinner. How about it?"

His forthright little speech drew another small laugh from her. "You're here for the weekend?" she asked, trying to fight off the disconcerting effect his eyes had on her.

"I've got a room reserved at an inn on Lake Waramaug, which is supposed to be somewhere around here."

"Just a couple of miles south," she told him. "I live on the lake myself."

"Fine. Will you join me for dinner?"

Emily wasn't the sort of woman who dated strangers. In this remote northwestern corner of Connecticut, she didn't date much at all. There weren't many eligible men around. Which suited her well enough, because she hadn't been particularly interested in meeting men since her divorce. But his eyes . . . She shook her head and gave yet another laugh, this one doubtful. "Lloyd Gordon, huh?"

"What's your name?"

"Emily Squires," she told him.

"Emily Squires," he murmured. "How about dinner?"

He certainly was persistent, she mused. So how about it? Dinner with a very handsome man. Why not? "Okay," she accepted. "But I've got to go home and change first."

"Obviously," he agreed. She wondered if she should be insulted by the remark, but he spoke again before she could react to it. "How do I find your house?"

"Take the road along the lake leading east from the New Preston town beach," she replied. "About a mile down. My house is on the left-hand side, across the street from the lake. It's a small yellow shack, actually. You'll see my mailbox at the driveway. 'Squires' in big red letters. You can't miss it."

"A small yellow shack," he repeated. "I'll pick you up in an hour."

"See you then," she said, tossing him a wide, dimpled grin as she headed for her car.

She was still grinning when she reached the center of New Preston, a tiny village nestled at the base of Lake Waramaug, and steered along the winding road paralleling the lake. Her pleasure at Lloyd Gordon's invitation for dinner surprised her. One of the reasons she liked her job at the animal clinic in Litchfield was that she didn't have to deal with many men in this region of small resorts and settled families. Although she'd recovered fully from her divorce, she wasn't interested in pursuing a new romance, and the Litchfield Hills offered few opportunities for one to develop.

She was a country girl; she liked the solitude and seclusion of the region, the blend of neighborly concern and Yankee aloofness the area's residents boasted. People kept to themselves here, they respected each other's privacy and didn't flaunt their personalities. It was a wholesome place, Emily believed, a place where a woman could be herself—and be *by* herself—without anyone interfering. A far cry from the life she'd been living in Los Angeles.

She drove up the bumpy, unpaved driveway to her ramshackle cottage and coasted into the detached garage beside it. As she climbed out of her car, she heard the enthusiastic barking of Gus welcoming her home. Hastening to the cluttered, overgrown backyard of her house, she was hailed by her rambunctious dog, whose lineage emphasized Labrador retriever with a few other breeds mixed in, standard poodle and Chesapeake retriever among them. Whatever he was, Gus was big. Only a year and a half old, he was already enormous, though he seemed unaware of his size as he romped and played like a puppy.

"Hello, Gus!" she greeted him as she unclipped the rope that connected his collar to a long runner cord on pulleys that she'd erected between two trees. Gus eagerly licked her hands as she unfastened the tether. As soon as he was free, he leaped up on her, planting his clumsy paws on her shoulders in an attempt to hug her.

"I'm glad to see you, too," she returned his warmth, scratching the short black fur behind his ears before racing him to her kitchen door. He powered past her, hurling his weight at the door, and she shook her head and laughed. He really was getting strong, she recognized. She'd have to buy a thicker rope for his runner leash.

She let him into the house, set down her purse on the kitchen table, and filled his food and water dishes for him. He exuberantly impeded her by running between her legs. When she finally set the two dishes on the sheets of newspaper she had spread on the floor in the corner of the room by the stove, he dove enthusiastically into his dinner. "Eat up, Gus," she urged him. "You're on your own tonight. I've got a date."

He ignored her, and she left the small kitchen. When she got around to it, she intended to lay down new flooring, and then maybe replace the archaic appliances with more modern ones. But the house needed more fundamental repairs before she turned her attention to cosmetic improvements. Besides being tiny, the cottage had been in dreadful condition when Emily had bought it, but that was the only way she could have afforded a lakeside house. Across the street from her was only a narrow strip of pebbly beach and a rickety boat dock she shared with two neighbors. The lake was practically hers.

Given its location, her house had cost much more than the structure warranted, but she loved it. She'd already reroofed the house, insulated it, and installed a new furnace. This weekend she planned to finish repairing the front porch where the wood had rotted in spots. The backyard needed to be cleared of a dead tree that had tumbled onto her property from the surrounding forest during a storm several weeks before, and the chimney of the wood-burning stove in the living room required cleaning before autumn. Emily would have to hire a specialist to do that, but she performed most of the other repairs herself. She was strong and capable. She liked being self-sufficient.

She wandered through the compact living room and past the second bedroom, which she'd converted into a den. In her own bedroom she undressed. Then she headed to the bathroom to shower. She took her time, scrubbing the faint smell of animals from her hands and hair. The bulk of her work at the clinic, which she ran with another veterinarian and an assistant, involved routine checkups of pets, giving them their shots, clipping their nails, spaying them, and attending to their minor ailments. Like her home, her current job was a far cry from the work she'd been doing in Los Angeles, where she'd been employed by a large agency that represented animals that performed in films and on television. Dealing with trained panthers and boa constrictors had been interesting, but deep in her heart Emily preferred dogs, cats, birds, and the animals that dwelled in the forests that spread through the Litchfield Hills.

Once she was finished showering, she blow-dried her red-blond hair and brushed it loose, letting it fall in glittering waves past her shoulders. Then she returned to her bedroom to choose something to wear. Most of the inns and restaurants along the lake were fairly elegant. And Lloyd Gordon, despite his casual attire, struck her as an elegant sort of person. Rich, anyway. That BMW must have cost a pretty penny.

After scrutinizing the contents of her closet, she selected a demure shirtwaist dress of dark blue cotton. It had long sleeves, which would probably be necessary; even in June the evenings were cool by the lake. She slipped on the dress, opened the top two buttons, and adjusted the collar about her throat. She studied herself in the full-length mirror attached to the back of her bedroom door. The dress flattered her body's ripe curves. It didn't make her look skinny, but then nothing ever would make her look skinny. Whether or not she went on a diet, she grumbled, she'd always look pinchably soft.

She heard Gus scratching on her closed door, and she swung it wide to admit him. He stared up at her, his moist brown eyes reflecting his apparent astonishment at her dressiness. Gus was used to seeing his mistress clad in jeans or shorts and T-shirts, not such feminine attire. "What do you think, Gussie?" Emily asked as she modeled her dress for him, pirouetting before her attentive pet. "Am I gonna knock Lloyd's socks off or what?" The dog panted energetically, and Emily laughed. "Hot date, pal. A new experience, huh?" Gus licked her knee through the sheer nylon of her stocking and she shoved him away. "Animal!" she chided him playfully.

Abruptly he flinched, then bolted from the room. Emily stepped out of her bedroom to see Gus scamper toward the front door, growling and yapping. She hadn't heard the doorbell, but she hurried to the front door and opened it in time to see Lloyd swinging out of his car. He wore a pair of dark gray slacks, a white shirt with its collar unbuttoned, and a gray tweed blazer. She switched on the porch light before lifting her eyes to his. They were just as glacial as she had remembered, just as startling, like two round chips of ice.

The smile he offered when their eyes met did nothing to quiet Emily's unexpected nervousness. He was gorgeous, she acknowledged, possibly the most handsome man she'd ever met. *Just visiting for the weekend,* she swiftly reminded herself. *Just a drink and dinner.* "Watch yourself on the porch steps," she cautioned him as he approached, and the smooth, welcoming sound of her voice calmed her slightly. "They're a little bit rotted toward the left."

He carefully picked his way up to the porch and entered the house. Before he could speak, Gus flung himself at Lloyd, slamming his ungainly paws against Lloyd's thighs and knocking him into the wall. Lloyd muttered an oath.

"Down, boy, down!" Emily scolded Gus, grabbing his collar and dragging him off Lloyd, who fastidiously dusted off his trousers and glared at the friendly mongrel. "Sorry," Emily apologized for her pet, though she couldn't stifle a laugh at Lloyd's obvious annoyance. "He's just a little frisky."

"A little frisky?" Lloyd scowled at Gus, who strained against Emily's hand. "The beast tried to kill me!"

Emily's laughter swelled. "Oh, come now. He was just saying hello."

"He ought to learn English," Lloyd grumbled, not at all amused.

"Come on, Gussie, down," Emily admonished her dog, stroking him soothingly behind his ears. His tongue lapped the air and his tail wagged cheerfully. He was clearly taken with her visitor. "Don't you like dogs?" Emily asked Lloyd.

"Not particularly," he replied.

Emily's smile waned. Not liking dogs was a definite strike against Lloyd Gordon. "Well, Gus likes you," she defended the dog. "He just hasn't gotten used to the fact that he isn't puppy-size anymore. Come on, Gus," she said, leading the dog toward the cellar stairs. "Lloyd doesn't like you. Hard to believe, isn't it?"

Gus evidently concurred. He cheerfully licked Emily's palm before trotting down the stairs to the basement.

Emily closed the door and turned to Lloyd. His eyes were fixed on her, their cool blue irises sparkling. "Hard to believe, eh?" he asked.

"In my book not liking dogs is hard to believe," she declared, striding to the kitchen to wash her hands. She dried them briskly on a dish towel and then passed Lloyd on her way to her bedroom to collect her purse. She resented his failure to return Gus's affection. Gus was harmless, for goodness sake, and someone as tall and manly as Lloyd certainly oughtn't to be afraid of a rowdy, overgrown puppy. If Lloyd really didn't like dogs, the evening just might turn out to be ghastly.

Drawing in a deep breath and determining to make the best of things, she returned to the living room to find Lloyd at the window, staring through the trees at the lake. "Shall we go?" she asked, struggling futilely to control the brusqueness in her tone.

He spun around, his acute gaze assessing her. "Are you one of these love-me-love-my-dog types?" he asked.

"I'm not a 'type,'" she countered stonily. "But Gus was only being friendly. A little friendliness never hurt anyone."

"Friendly?" Lloyd snorted. "He practically knocked me off my feet."

"He's high-spirited," Emily said, tautly defending Gus.

"High-spirited? He's completely wild!"

"Are you saying I haven't trained him properly?" Emily bristled.

"Well, he's lacking in manners."

"So are you!" she exploded. "If you don't know how to accept a little well-intended love, a little warmth, a little healthy energy . . ."

Something in Lloyd's expression made her trail off. In the fading evening light, his face was half in shadow, but his eyes cut through the descending gloom, piercing the darkness, stabbing Emily. She couldn't decipher their strange light, but it intrigued her. She no longer wanted to defend her dog to Lloyd. She no longer wanted to fight with him. She wanted only to understand his eyes. She wanted to come to terms with the guarded power of them. They were beautiful eyes, beautiful but hard. She wanted to thaw them. She wanted to reach past them, to find the man hiding behind them. She was astounded by the yearning they awakened in her, but there it was.

"Are you done?" he asked coolly. "Can we go now?"

I'm not done, Emily silently answered. His sudden reserve didn't discourage her. Like his eyes, it fascinated her. She was curious about Lloyd Gordon.

She tossed him a pleasant smile and preceded him through the door, locking it once he'd joined her outside. Her smile deepened as he helped her into the passenger seat of his car and then strolled around to the driver's side. He glanced at her before starting the engine, and her smile seemed to amaze him. Almost in spite of himself, he matched it, his mouth curving into a tenuous grin.

Emily settled back against the plush, leather upholstery. A small laugh lodged in her throat, but she tactfully swallowed it. For some reason she couldn't help suspecting that Lloyd *did* like dogs. All his temper and bluster didn't mean a thing. Lloyd liked dogs, and Emily knew it.

2

Lake Waramaug was long and narrow, cutting an east-to-west S-shape through the rolling Litchfield Hills. The inn to which Lloyd drove sat on the lake's northern shore, almost directly across the water from Emily's house. He parked in an unpaved lot beside a sprawling farmhouse that evidently dated back to the previous century. It had been beautifully restored. Its shingled walls were painted a fresh white, its shutters and trim black; its brick chimneys stood clean and straight. The wraparound porch was nearly hidden behind the dense flowering shrubbery of rhododendron and azaleas, displaying their vivid pink blooms.

After locking his car, Lloyd escorted Emily inside the building, through a small parlor decorated with colonial antiques and into a paneled dining room. An attractive young hostess greeted them and ushered them to a table on a jalousied dining porch adjacent to the main dining area.

"Is this where you're staying?" Emily asked as she took a seat beside the open window, facing Lloyd. A ceiling fan drew air laden with the perfume of blossoms through the open window slats and into the enclosed porch.

Lloyd nodded in reply. Emily briefly wondered whether he intended to take her to his room after dinner. If he invited her, she would refuse. She couldn't deny his good looks, his magnificent physique and appealing face. She couldn't deny the urge to run her fingers through the thick black curls that framed it, or to brush her mouth over the soft mustache that covered his upper lip. But she wouldn't go to his room with him. Not only because she hardly knew him, but because she didn't see the point of it. Even after knowing Ed for seven years, the last two of which they'd spent married, she'd never found much satisfaction in sex. She definitely wasn't interested in experimenting with a complete stranger who happened to be in town for the weekend.

A waitress arrived at their table and asked if they wanted cocktails. Lloyd eyed Emily. "Gin and tonic," she requested.

"A gin and tonic and a Bloody Mary," he ordered. The waitress departed.

Emily settled back in her chair and studied Lloyd across the table, which had been set with a pink linen tablecloth and featured a crystal bud vase holding a delicate arrangement of ferns and miniature daisies. Lloyd returned her steady gaze, his eyes cool and emotionless, though his lips hinted at a smile. "So," she said spiritedly. "Tell me about yourself."

His smile expanded slightly, not quite reaching his eyes. "What do you want to know?"

"Where are you from?"

"Hartford."

"That's not far from here," she observed. "Do you vacation in the area often?"

"No," Lloyd answered.

She couldn't decide whether his tone was curt or merely shy. Undeterred, she forged ahead. "Where do you usually take your vacations?"

"I don't," he replied.

"You don't what?"

"I don't take vacations," he declared.

The waitress carried their drinks to the table, and Emily accepted hers with a nod. "Maybe we ought to drink a toast to vacations, then," she suggested once the waitress had deposited two menus and vanished.

Lloyd offered only a pensive half smile before lifting his glass toward Emily and then drinking.

Emily took a small sip of her gin and tonic, feeling the bubbles fizz and burst on her tongue as she considered Lloyd's enigmatic reaction to her toast. "You don't like vacations, I take it," she hazarded.

"I didn't say that," Lloyd replied. "I just don't take them. Often. I'm here, though, aren't I?"

"For the weekend," she recalled. "One weekend. That hardly counts. When was the last time you took a real vacation?"

He gave the question more thought than it deserved before saying, "Five years ago."

"*Five years ago?*" she repeated in disbelief. "What are you, a workaholic or something?"

His mouth flexed, but he remained silent, his eyes growing almost imperceptibly chillier as he took another long sip from his glass.

Emily contemplated the veil that had dropped over his face, marking the distance he seemed to be laboring to maintain from her. Was he hiding something, she wondered, or did he simply think she was being a busybody? With a small shrug, she decided she didn't care what he thought. He'd asked her out, after all. He must have assumed she'd be curious about him. They had to talk about something. "What sort of work do you do?" she asked.

"Economic forecasting," he told her.

"Do you work for the government?" Emily didn't know much about economic forecasting, but since Hartford was the state capital, she assumed the question was reasonable.

"I used to," he answered. "I've got my own consulting firm now. We do research for the government, as well as for private industry. The insurance companies use us a lot."

Emily nodded; in addition to being Connecticut's capital, Hartford also housed a large number of corporate headquarters for insurance companies. She took heart in Lloyd's having answered her question with more than a few terse words, and she dared to probe further. "Your firm must require a lot of attention if you can't take a vacation more often than once every five years."

Again he seemed to withdraw from her, his eyes glinting metallically and his lips freezing into a straight line. He fingered his glass, his frosty gaze fixed on Emily, and considered his words before speaking. "I don't take vacations because I don't want to. I'm not even sure I wanted to take this one. But here I am. Let's order, shall we?" Before Emily could respond, he lifted his menu and opened it.

She stared numbly at the list of entrees before her, her brain scrambling to make sense of Lloyd's icy detachment. If he didn't want to talk to her, if he didn't want to make amiable conversation with her, why had he asked her to join him for dinner? His reticence grated on her. She was willing to respect people's privacy—in fact, she preferred Lloyd's reserve to the cloying effusiveness she had found among the kind of people she and Ed had known in southern California. But the secretive shell Lloyd erected about himself irked her. Or maybe it wasn't his mood that irked her so much as her desire to penetrate that shell. She usually *wasn't* a busybody, but Lloyd piqued her curiosity. His subtle rebuffing of her innocuous attempts at conversation rankled.

When the waitress came to take their orders, Emily requested Steak Diane and Lloyd Veal Cordon Bleu. The waitress departed once more, and Emily confronted Lloyd. "You know, you don't have to be so rude," she accused him.

His eyes glittered with an enigmatic silver light. "Rude?"

"Rude. I think I'm asking pretty innocent questions. It's not like I'm prying into your finances or taking your fingerprints. Honestly, Lloyd, if you don't want to talk to me, you can take me home. I'll just chalk it up to the fact that you're unsociable and forget about it."

He continued his perusal of her, angling his head slightly as he meditated. He was neither smiling nor frowning; his expression was totally unreadable to Emily. "Unsociable?" he finally managed.

"Well, what would you call it? First you insult Gus, then you say you haven't taken a vacation in five years, and then you act huffy and snippy when all I'm trying to do is get to know you a little better." Her dark eyes matched his in flintiness, and her chin poked slightly forward, daring him to refute her assessment of him. "If that's not unsociable, I don't know what is."

He looked as if he were about to smile, but his mouth resisted, curving only the slightest bit at the corners. "Maybe I just think you're a little nosy," he commented.

"Okay, mister," Emily muttered. "You lay out the safe territories, and I'll try to stick to them."

The smile won out, arching his reluctant lips. He leaned back in his chair, still observing Emily speculatively. A soft, husky chuckle rose from his chest. "I'll tell you what," he proposed. "You fire away, and when you're out of bounds, I'll let you know."

She wasn't sure his suggestion pleased her. Apparently he *did* think she was a busybody, and he *was* put off by her simple questions. But he wasn't demanding that she stop. In fact, he seemed to be obliquely encouraging her to continue asking him about himself. She saw the waitress approaching with their soup, and waited until they were alone again before saying, "You think I'm nosy, huh?"

"A little," Lloyd confirmed, stirring his clam chowder and tasting a spoonful.

"What would you like to talk about?" she said, politely deferring to him.

Once again he seemed to give her question more thought than it required. "You," he responded.

All right, Emily thought. She'd show him how to be courteous and civil and friendly. "Anything." She pretended an exaggerated welcome of his interest in her. "My life's an open book."

He laughed. "How long have you lived here?" he asked.

"A couple of years," Emily replied after swallowing a mouthful of cold cucumber soup.

"And before that?"

"L.A.," she told him.

His eyebrows inched up. "Forgive me for sounding provincial and bigoted, but I'd never have guessed you were from Los Angeles."

"Oh?" Her eyes twinkled with amusement. "Why not?"

"You seem too . . . natural," he commented, then shook his head. "That does sound provincial and bigoted, doesn't it?"

"What do you mean by 'natural'?" she pressed him.

He lowered his eyes to his soup and twirled his spoon

thoughtfully through the creamy broth. "Easterners have all sorts of strange conceptions about Southern Californians," he confessed. "Flaky, showy, cocaine addicts, wife-swappers, Beautiful People, and all that."

"Some of the above," Emily granted. At his sharp glance, she clarified her comment. "Not me, but some of the people I knew out there were like that. I don't miss California."

"How did you get from there to here?"

"After I got my divorce there wasn't any reason to stay," she frankly told him, silently adding, *See? An open book.*

He appeared surprised by her revelation. "You're divorced?"

"That's one you forgot in your little list about Southern Californians. I think it falls between wife-swappers and Beautiful People. Divorced." She finished her soup and set down her spoon.

"You don't seem terribly bitter," he observed.

"I'm not," Emily asserted with a dimpled smile. "I'm much more satisfied with my life now than I was then. Why should I be bitter?"

Their soup bowls were removed and their salads delivered. As soon as the waitress was gone, Lloyd turned his attention back to Emily. He seemed as fascinated by her candor as he was by what she was saying. "Were you a vet out there?" he asked, sounding genuinely interested.

"I worked for a company that supplied acting animals to show biz," she related. "For instance, if someone wanted to film a television commercial and they needed three orangutans for it, they'd call up my boss, and he'd supply the orangs. He had a bunch of vets working for him, keeping the menagerie in good health. It was a bizarre job," she allowed with a laugh. "Good experience, but not the sort of thing I'd want to make my life's career."

"Did your husband work with animals too?" Lloyd asked.

Emily laughed again. "In a manner of speaking," she granted. "He's an actor. Doing quite well, too. His name is Ed Bonneville. He's a regular on one of the prime-time soaps. Maybe you've heard of him."

Lloyd shook his head. "I don't watch much television."

"Neither do I," Emily admitted. "Occasionally I'll tune in to see how Eddie's doing, but usually I'd rather read a good book or play with Gus."

Lloyd gave her a lengthy appraisal, ignoring the waitress when she brought their entrees to the table. "An actor's wife in Hollywood," he murmured. "You just don't seem the type, Emily."

"Did I just catch another whiff of that East-Coast bigotry?" Emily mocked him, then relented with a gentle laugh. "You're right. I'm not the type. When Eddie and I met in college, he dreamed of working as a stage actor at some low-key regional theater. He did just that while I finished veterinary school. And then, a couple of months after we got married, out of the blue he decided to audition for this awful television show. He got the part, and suddenly there we were in Hollywood, being Beautiful People and flaky and all those things. At least he was. He enjoyed that kind of life much more than I did." She shrugged. "So I left."

"You make it sound very simple," Lloyd commented quietly.

Well, it hadn't been quite as simple as Emily made it sound, she acknowledged privately. First there had been Ed's demands that she change, that she lose some weight and lighten her hair and try to be more glamorous, like the women he worked with. And when Emily refused to try to be something she couldn't be, there had been Ed's infidelities. The first one had been a shock, a disappointment, a sharp blow to Emily's ego.

The second had inspired her to sue for divorce. But Emily had outgrown her hurt and anger long ago. She missed the person Ed had been when he was a student and then an unaffected actor at the repertory theater in Syracuse. But he'd changed, and she didn't miss the man he had become.

Lloyd ate in silence for a while, and Emily also concentrated on her food. She wondered whether Lloyd was put off by the fact that she was divorced, or merely by her candor. A little candor wouldn't hurt him, she decided—he could use some opening up himself. As far as her divorce went, well, it was a fact. There wasn't much she could do about it. If he didn't like it, that was his tough luck.

"Food's good here," she commented after tasting her Steak Diane, steamed asparagus, and cheese-stuffed potato. "For your first vacation in five years, you could have done worse."

"I suppose I could have," he agreed. He again lapsed into silence for several minutes, then set down his silverware and polished off his Bloody Mary. "What made you decide to become a vet?" he asked.

She was heartened by his willingness to resume a friendly dialogue. "I love animals," she replied.

"That's obvious. You really went nuts over that stupid deer."

"What makes you think he was stupid?" she argued, then grinned sheepishly. "I'll grant you, a deer doesn't have the intellect of a human being, but by eminent domain he probably has more right to be romping around the area than your car does. Most animals can't smell automobiles. They aren't aware of the danger until it's too late."

"Are there many deer around here?"

Emily nodded. "Sometimes, if I wake up very early, when the earth is half asleep and Gus is snoozing, I'll spy a deer grazing in my backyard. They seem completely unaware of civilization, and they're so peaceful and graceful. It's the most beautiful sight in the world." She sighed. "You don't see deer grazing in your yard in the Los Angeles suburbs. It's no wonder I don't miss that place."

"They are beautiful creatures," Lloyd concurred. Emily felt a small thrill of triumph ripple through her. He did like animals, after all.

When they had finished their meal, they topped it off with dessert and coffee. Lloyd seemed to have relaxed somewhat with her, though that might have been because she'd stopped asking him personal questions. She preferred to think it was because he'd grown more comfortable with her. She really shouldn't care, but she did. She was still undeniably curious about him, a man with such inscrutable eyes, a man who never took vacations. She sensed pain in him, a deeply buried pain, something unspoken in need of healing. It was the same pain she occasionally saw in her patients, animals unable to verbalize what was ailing them. The urge to break through to Lloyd, to locate his pain and heal it, was not unlike the urge to cure the animals she worked with every day.

It was an odd understanding, and she sternly reminded herself that Lloyd was only visiting for the weekend. He would be gone in a couple of days, out of her life. Whatever his reasons were for asking her to join him for dinner, she suspected that they didn't include a quick dose of veterinary treatment.

He set his empty coffee cup in its porcelain saucer and gave Emily a cool look. "Would you like to come up to my room?" he asked.

She'd wanted candor; she'd gotten it. Crimson flashed along her high cheekbones, though his question wasn't unexpected. "No," she answered softly. "I'd rather not."

He didn't register anger or even disappointment. She

expected him to offer to take her home, but instead he said, "Why don't we take a walk by the lake, then?"

"All right." She was more than relieved by his suggestion. She hadn't been ready to say good-bye to him yet. Once more she reminded herself that he was only a temporary visitor, but even so she refused to stifle her fascination with him. She was glad he wanted to extend their evening together.

He signed the bill, jotting down his room number. Then he helped Emily from her chair and strolled with her through the dining room and outside. The sky was clear and dark, speckled with pinpoints of starlight, and the air was balmy. Lloyd slipped Emily's hand through the bend of his arm as they ambled across a sloping lawn, past a clay tennis court and several small bungalows, and down to the waterfront. Part of the inn's shoreline was marked off as a beach. Lloyd steered her to a cozy patio beside the beach area, where half a dozen wrought-iron chairs were clustered. He drew two together, and indicated with a gesture that she should sit.

He took his seat beside her, then turned his gaze to the placid black water of the lake. The lights of houses and docks on the opposite shore were reflected by the motionless surface of the water. "Can we see your house from here?" he asked.

"I don't think so," Emily replied, leaning forward in her chair and studying the curves of the shoreline. "I'm just beyond that bend," she said, pointing out the arching coast to him. He nodded.

Leaning back, Emily felt Lloyd's arm slung over her chair, and it slid casually around her shoulders when she settled herself into the seat. His arm felt strong without being imposing. She suspected that if she asked him to remove it he would. But she didn't ask. She liked the feel of it, the warmth and comfort it provided. "Are you mad that I wouldn't go to your room?" she asked.

He tilted his head to study her, then grinned. "Not really," he confessed. "I think I would have been surprised if you'd said yes."

"Thought you'd just give it the old college try and see what happened, huh?" she teased him.

He chuckled, a deep, smoky laugh that warmed Emily as much as his arm about her. He ought to laugh more often, she mused. She had the feeling that he laughed about as frequently as he apologized—not very often at all. She was gratified way out of proportion that she'd succeeded in getting him to do both in one day.

A small motorboat glided through the water not far from them, its taillight illuminating its frothing wake. "The lake's lovely, isn't it?" she murmured.

Lloyd nodded.

"You ought to come here more often," she remarked, realizing at once that he could easily misconstrue her comment. She covered her forwardness by asking, "Where did you take your last vacation?"

"Here," he answered, astounding her.

"Here?"

"Not at this inn," he told her. His voice seemed hesitant and strangely hoarse. "We rented a cottage down the road a way."

"We?"

"My wife and I."

Wife? "You're divorced too?" she asked.

"Widowed," he said, so softly she had to strain to hear him.

Widowed. Was that the pain she detected in him? Was that the pain that he wrapped around himself like a cocoon, that caused the icy hardness in his eyes? Slowly the pieces fell into place. The last vacation he'd taken was here, with his wife—and then she'd died and he hadn't taken another vacation since. That he had chosen to return here seemed terribly significant to

Emily. She was filled with questions, but all she said was, "I'm sorry."

His gaze fixed on the water, he didn't speak. The only sound was the gentle lapping of the tide against the shore. Emily wasn't immediately aware of his fingers moving along her arm. She felt an eerie tension in her stomach, and then the gentle motion of his hand, drawing a line up to her shoulder before capturing a silky lock of her hair and combing through it in search of her neck. Her skin tingled as he brushed his fingers beneath the heavy fall of her red-gold tresses, but the tingling was superseded by the tautness in her abdomen, a reaction she'd never felt from a man's touch before. "May I kiss you?" he whispered.

She turned to him, unable to shape a reply in words. He clearly found the answer he wanted in her wide, dark eyes. His head bent to hers, and he covered her mouth with his own.

She had no intention of allowing his kiss to overwhelm her. She kept her eyes open, watching his face until it was too close to see, concentrating on the tickly sensation of his mustache against her upper lip. But her effort to resist the powerful surge of heat that welled within her was in vain. Dark frissons of desire spread from her mouth downward, heating her flesh, softening her. Her lids grew heavy and her lips pliant, submitting with astonishing eagerness to the advance of his tongue.

When her mouth opened he entered it, and her breath emerged in a throaty moan. She was vaguely aware of his thumb venturing beneath the collar of her dress, exploring her creamy skin as his fingers wove possessively through her hair, holding her head steady. His tongue captured hers, captivated it, teased it with gentle thrusts before withdrawing to entice the inner flesh of her lips. Then it moved deep into her mouth again, tasting her essence, sipping her flavor. Her eyes closed as she surrendered totally to Lloyd's potent kiss.

He wrapped his other arm about her, pressing her body to his, ignoring the constraints of the chairs on which they sat. Her breasts collided with the unyielding surface of his chest, and as if no layers of cloth separated her from Lloyd, she felt her nipples stiffen with fiery life at the contact. She wondered what his body would look like, how it would feel. Her hands lifted to touch him, feeding her wonder as they satisfied it. She slid her fingers beneath the tweedy wool of his blazer, then ran them across the crisp fabric of his shirt, discerning the strength of his shoulders before traveling down to his chest. Her fingertips visualized what her eyes couldn't see.

This wasn't like her at all, Emily thought as Lloyd's hand drifted down to her waist and back up her spine, as his tongue invited hers to conquer his mouth as he'd conquered hers. It wasn't like her to respond to a strange man. Or to any man, for that matter. She'd always enjoyed kissing and holding Ed, but her body had never transcended mere enjoyment. Even at the beginning of her relationship with Ed, when he'd been faithful and devoted to her, she'd been unable to react to his sexual forays with anything other than a superficial pleasure. Sometimes she'd experienced the inkling of a more explosive passion lurking within her, but it never went anywhere, and she'd assumed she simply wasn't a very passionate person. Ed had used a harsher term to describe her lack of sexual response, and in moments of total honesty, she'd believed he was right.

But now she wasn't so sure. One kiss from Lloyd was almost enough to convince her that her body was capable of feelings she hadn't known before. Almost enough, she sighed, retreating slightly, letting her hands fall to his knees and then hastily to her own as she remembered the unique frustration she'd felt on those occasions with Ed when her flesh had hinted at success, had tantalized her with a promise that was never fulfilled. Lloyd was an expert kisser, but years of disappointment convinced Emily that she'd fail in his arms as completely as she had failed with her husband.

He felt her pulling away from him, and his embrace loosened slightly, though he didn't release her. He inched his face from hers and stared at her, his penetrating eyes absorbing her confused expression. He seemed on the verge of speaking, then changed his mind and pressed his lips together.

"Please don't ask me to your room again," Emily murmured, her breath uneven, her breasts rising and falling spasmodically against the bodice of her dress.

"Afraid you might say yes?" Lloyd asked with a tentative smile.

Afraid of much more than that, Emily silently acknowledged. "I wouldn't," she said, too quickly.

He continued to study her, his eyes clear but his thoughts hidden. "You're very beautiful," he told her. It sounded more like a simple evaluation than an attempt to flatter her into changing her mind.

"I'm fat," she argued.

"What?" He seemed taken aback.

"I'm big and lumpy. I'm built like a cow."

He gaped at her, leaning away, searching her face for a sign that she was joking. "What are you talking about? You've got a beautiful figure."

"You like a 'full-figured' woman, is that it?"

He didn't smile. "I like . . ." He paused to reflect. "I like a woman who looks like the wind won't blow her away," he said slowly.

"Hmm," she acknowledged skeptically. "I've survived a few tornadoes and here I am."

"Here you are," he breathed, bowing his head to kiss her again.

The mere sight of his mouth's approach caused the muscles in her abdomen to contract almost painfully. She clamped her teeth against her lips to seal them and recoiled from Lloyd. "No," she groaned, pushing herself to her feet and marching toward the water's edge.

He followed her, and when she risked turning to him she saw the guarded coldness in his eyes. It convinced her that she was correct in refusing his kiss. Although he said nothing, his grim expression elicited an agitated explanation from her. "What the hell do you want from me? You're a tourist, for crying out loud. Just passing through. What are you looking for, a willing lady to entertain you for the weekend? Forget it."

She spun back to the water, resenting its lovely tranquillity. Her emotions resembled a turbulent storm at sea. She wanted to see ten-foot waves crashing against the earth, spraying the sky with violent foam.

When Lloyd finally spoke, his voice was so soft it almost seemed a part of the dark night air around them. "I'm not looking for anything," he asserted.

The quiet force of his words persuaded Emily of their truth. She felt a trembling in her limbs as she let Lloyd's statement resonate within her. He wasn't looking for *anything*, not a weekend's entertainment, not the meaning of life, not happiness or contentment. Not anything at all. When she dared to face him again, her face registered contrition. She'd overreacted to his disturbing kiss, and she had no right to inflict her bewilderment and anger on him. She suddenly felt horribly sorry, sorry not only for directing her rage at him but for his own inability or unwillingness to search for anything. "Why?" she asked.

He seemed perplexed. "Why what?"

"Why aren't you looking for anything?"

His puzzlement blended with impatience. "Oh, Emily," he grumbled. "Are you going to play games with me? You said no; I assume you meant it. If you meant something else, spit it out."

"I didn't mean that you should look for something with me," she struggled to explain herself. "I meant

39

. . . I meant you should look for *something*. You should open up, Lloyd, break out, stop hiding." It occurred to her that she had no right to say such things to him, but Emily *didn't* play games, and her tactlessness proved as much to Lloyd.

"Stop hiding?" The strange, hard glint of his gaze was laced with curiosity. "What makes you think I'm hiding?"

Emily lowered her eyes to the grass beneath their feet. It had been neatly mowed, cropped as close as the pile of a soft green carpet. She focused on Lloyd's black loafers, and her own open-toed pumps. "You are," she insisted, wondering if she sounded rash, wondering if Lloyd considered her insufferably rude. Yet she was unable to stifle her concern. "You're as cold as ice, and then you kiss me and—" She drifted off, unsure of how to continue.

"And?" he goaded her.

"And I know you aren't ice," she concluded weakly.

He took a moment to mull over her words. "What am I?" he probed.

"You tell me."

He considered again, then slipped his hand beneath her chin and steered her eyes back to his. "I'm a man," he declared.

"And you want a lady to entertain you for the weekend?"

"And I want . . ." He took a deep, steady breath. "I want to see you tomorrow."

She hadn't expected him to say that. She'd expected him to imply that he wanted to see her, preferably in his bed and naked. But his statement indicated that he was more than willing to back off, to respect the limits she'd established without questioning them.

She wanted to see him, too. She wanted to spend her Saturday with him, to learn more about him, to learn more about the man who could awaken such unfamiliar sensations inside her with his kiss. "I can't," she announced glumly as she sorted her thoughts. "I've got to do some work on my house tomorrow. It's falling apart, as you've probably noticed."

"What sort of work?" he asked.

"I was going to repair the porch steps."

"I could help."

Her eyes flashed darkly. "You're on vacation, Lloyd. You shouldn't be spending your weekend patching up a handyman's special."

He shrugged. "It'll go faster if we work on it together."

He was serious. A bemused grin twisted her lips. "You really want to work on my porch?"

"You probably look pretty silly with nails sticking out of your mouth," he teased. "I wouldn't want to miss that."

"I never put nails in my mouth. It's unsafe," she asserted, then shrugged. "Suit yourself, Lloyd. I'll be at it all day, if you want to drop by and pitch in."

"I do," he insisted. His smile faded, and his hand slid to her cheek. He touched his mouth to hers, and the tender kiss seared her lips, another shock to her system, and to her sensibility. Maybe she *should* stuff her mouth with nails, she mused. It might be safer than letting this man with his haunting eyes kiss her again.

"I'll take you home," he offered, as if he could read her mind.

Grateful for his discretion, she strolled with him up the grassy slope to the parking lot beside the inn. He could work with her on her porch tomorrow, if that was really what he wanted to do. But right now she thought it best to be alone, to regain her equilibrium. Lloyd Gordon did stimulate her curiosity, she conceded. And curiosity could be a very dangerous thing.

3

What can I say, Gus? He intrigues me."

Gus stretched his jaws in an exaggerated yawn. Emily had tied him to one of the vertical beams supporting the roof's overhang. He sat on the ground beside the four steps leading to the porch, watching his mistress organize herself for her task.

She had already lugged the pine boards she needed from her garage, where she'd been storing them. Then she'd carried the necessary tools up from her basement. Dressed in a pair of cutoff jeans and a pale blue work shirt, the tails of which she'd tied around her midriff, her feet bare and her hair pulled back into a ponytail, she was ready to begin her repair work on the porch.

The Saturday morning air was already warm, the sun bright, and the sky cloudless, but the front yard of her house was mercifully shaded by the foliage of the trees surrounding it. She lifted a crowbar and attacked the rotted board on the top step, jimmying it up without much effort.

Gus watched her with mild interest, and she continued to describe Lloyd to him. One of the things she liked best about Gus was his willingness to listen to her whenever she felt like talking. That, plus his inability to quarrel with her, made him an ideal companion.

"He's very handsome," she told Gus as she tossed the rotted plank aside. "Of course you know that; you've already met him. He has incredible eyes. But he's strange. Kind of like a clam, if you know what I mean. What do you think, Gussie? Is he worth breaking open?"

Gus yawned again and shifted his body into a shadow. He rested his head on his paws and eyed Emily soulfully.

"You don't think so, huh," she said, interpreting his expression. "I know, he's only here for the weekend. It's not worth it, getting involved with him. You're right. But . . ."

She wedged the claw end of her hammer beneath a rusted nail and pried it free. Her thoughts drifted from her manual labor to the evening she'd spent with Lloyd. Logically she knew there was no point in allowing a relationship to develop. He'd be gone tomorrow. Why bother trying to open him up?

Because of his kiss, she answered herself. Because of the way she'd felt in his arms. Because when his stunning eyes met hers, she'd read torment in them, sadness, something that made her long to reach him and console him. It was an irrational longing, but she couldn't deny it. Nor could she deny her suspicion that Lloyd wanted her to reach him, wanted her to open him up. She was unable to pinpoint precisely what gave her that impression, but somehow, subliminally, she understood that he wanted her to break through the shell surrounding him.

Gus heard the distant sound of an automobile's motor on the road bordering the lake before Emily did. He leaped to his feet and barked loudly. Glancing up, she spotted a gleaming black car through the trees. It navigated the bend, then slowed and turned up her driveway. Braking to a halt, Lloyd switched off his engine and climbed out of the car.

He had on the same jeans he'd been wearing the previous day, when Emily had first met him, and a green cotton polo shirt that hugged his lean chest. His eyes glinted like diamonds beneath his lids, which were lowered against the sun's glare. His lips curved in a lazy smile as he approached Emily.

Gus galloped toward the visitor, straining against his tether. Lloyd backed up a step, remaining beyond the range of Gus's leash, and scowled at the exuberant dog. "Call him off, will you?" he ordered Emily.

She laughed at Lloyd's churlishness. "He isn't *on*," she pointed out. "Why should I call him off?"

Still scowling, Lloyd moved in a wide circle toward the porch, avoiding Gus as best he could. "I don't like being hugged by creatures that are bigger than I am," he explained coldly.

"He's harmless," Emily insisted, sliding her fingers beneath Gus's collar and ushering him to Lloyd, who curled his lip as he peered down at the affable mutt. Gus returned his gaze, his eyes brimming with hopeful excitement and his tail swishing vigorously, though he refrained from jumping on Lloyd. "Come on, pet him," Emily urged Lloyd. "He's such a sweetheart, how can you not love him?"

Lloyd's frown intensified, but he reluctantly extended his hand and ruffled the fur between Gus's floppy ears. Gus issued a cheerful bark in thanks.

"See? He's crazy about you," Emily claimed.

"Well, I'm not crazy about him," Lloyd said, turning his attention to the dismantled porch steps. His tone softened as he observed, "You've already started. I should have gotten here earlier."

"Don't be silly." Emily brushed off his apology. "You're on vacation. You're supposed to sleep late."

"What do you want me to do?"

She surveyed her equipment and shrugged. "I'm going to pry up the rest of these rotting planks. The underside structure looks good, so we'll just have to hammer on some new boards. Why don't you measure them for sawing?"

He eyed the steps, then the new lumber. "Why don't you measure and I'll pry?" he gallantly offered.

Emily considered telling him that she was fully capable of prying up the old boards herself, but she realized that she didn't have to defend her ability to him. He could see by what she'd already accomplished that she wasn't a weakling. With an easy smile, she agreed to his division of the chores.

He hoisted the crowbar and attacked the steps while she gathered up her tape measure, pencil, and straightedge to mark off the correct lengths on the new wood. She frequently glanced up to watch Lloyd work. His shoulders flexed powerfully beneath the cotton knit of his shirt, but his hands were so smooth that she couldn't help assuming that he rarely engaged in manual labor. "Do you often do repairs at your house?" she asked.

He shook his head, then levered the bar beneath a plank. "I live in an apartment," he replied. "The building has a maintenance staff."

"Do you mind doing this?"

"It's a change of pace," he answered noncommittally.

Well, if he minded, he wouldn't have volunteered to help, she surmised. She finished marking the boards and heaved them onto a strong part of the porch. Then she grasped her saw, knelt on the first board to hold it steady, and began an even cut at the line she'd drawn.

He stopped working to watch her. "Do you want me to do that?" he asked.

She chuckled indulgently. "I'm not helpless, Lloyd. I've sawed wood before." Her efficient strokes with the saw offered evidence of her skill and experience.

"In Los Angeles?"

"In Kansas," she told him.

"Kansas?" He sounded surprised.

She lifted her gaze to his. His eyes were as hard and unreadable as ever, but she detected curiosity in their glittering depths. "That's where I grew up," she informed him. "Bellewood, Kansas."

"Bellewood?"

"You've never heard of it," she guessed. "It's a very small town. Blink and you've passed it."

"Are you a farm girl?"

"Almost," she admitted. "Bellewood's a farming community, but I lived in town. All my friends grew up on farms, though. I've seen the inside of more than one corncrib in my day." The saw cut cleanly through the board, and the measured length dropped neatly onto the ground.

Lloyd watched her as she lined up the board to make a second cut. He was smiling, not the indolent smile he'd worn when he arrived, but a deeper, more appreciative smile that spread warmth through Emily. She returned the smile, her freckled cheeks dimpling, and he bent to his work again.

As the morning edged toward noon, the air grew warmer. Emily used her sleeves to mop her brow, then rolled them to her elbows. By the time Lloyd had finished removing the decayed steps, she had completed sawing the lumber, and they worked together to hammer the planks into place. They spoke little, their attention focused on the job. Emily wondered if he was enjoying himself. If she were on a vacation, she wouldn't want to spend her time repairing a porch. But

Lloyd didn't complain. He seemed exhilarated by his physical exertion. Emily reminded herself that such labor was a rarity for him, as rare as his vacation itself, perhaps. Obviously he was long overdue for a change of pace, and fixing her porch provided the change he needed.

By early afternoon they were done, and Emily silently acknowledged that the job had been completed much more quickly with Lloyd's assistance than it would have been if she'd tackled it alone. "Are you hungry?" she asked.

He shook his head.

"How about some lemonade? I for one am dying of thirst," she announced as Lloyd settled himself wearily onto one of the new steps and mopped his damp cheeks with the hem of his shirt.

In her kitchen she prepared a pitcher of lemonade, filled two tumblers with ice, and poured the drink into them. She carried the glasses out to the porch and found Lloyd and Gus studying each other, Lloyd wary and Gus stretching his lips in a canine version of a smile.

Emily grinned and dropped onto the step beside Lloyd. She handed him a glass and he took a long swallow. Lowering the glass, he exhaled. "You're exhausted," she noted.

He shook his head again. Tiny beads of perspiration trapped in the curls of black hair along the collar of his shirt caught the sun and sparkled. "I'm fine," he declared.

"I can't thank you enough for helping me," she murmured. "That was really kind of you, Lloyd."

He brusquely waved off her thanks. She sensed that her gratitude made him uncomfortable, though she didn't know why it should. But she respected his apparent uneasiness and fell silent, sipping the tart lemonade and then pressing the cold glass against her perspiring face.

"Kansas," he mused, gazing out at the lake. "Did you meet your husband in one of those corncribs?"

An amused laugh escaped her. "No, we met in college," she revealed. "Cornell. He was a city boy—or I guess a suburb boy, though the Long Island suburbs seemed like cities to me, compared with where I grew up." She sipped again, the ice cubes in her glass clicking against her teeth. "How about you?" she asked. "City boy?"

Lloyd nodded. "Manhattan."

"Did you meet your wife on a subway train?"

He stiffened, a muscle in his jaw twitching and his eyes remaining resolutely on the water. "I don't want to talk about her," he declared softly.

He was closing up again, Emily realized, closing up and shrinking from her. She chose to respect his mood. "So you grew up in New York, huh," she remarked. "I suppose people don't keep pet dogs in a crowded city."

"Some do." Lloyd shrugged, his detachment waning a little. "Little dogs, though. Lap dogs. Miniature poodles and Pekingese. They look like overgrown rats."

"I like big dogs myself," Emily said, unnecessarily. Lloyd glanced at Gus, whose enormous black body was curled in a crescent, his gangly legs tucked beneath him as he dozed in a patch of sunlight. "They don't yap so much."

"No. They growl," he grunted.

"Admit it," Emily goaded him. "You like Gus."

Lloyd refused to concede. "He's gross."

"Gross?" Emily's face registered annoyance.

"Gross in its original definition," Lloyd said justifying himself. "Big and unwieldy. Overbearing."

"I take it you like those fancy, groomed show animals who heel and turn their noses up at the world," Emily muttered.

"I don't like dogs much at all," Lloyd maintained.

"Do you like cats?"

"I don't like any pets," he stated, his voice strangely harsh. "They require too much time and attention. You have to take care of them; they're completely dependent on you." He angled his face to Emily. "What if you wanted to take a vacation? You're stuck with him."

"I'm not stuck," Emily insisted. "My partner, Tom, and his wife take him while I'm away. They've got a big house up in Litchfield, with two adopted strays of their own. When they go on vacation, I look after Taffy and Binkie. And when I go away, they look after Gus. It's no big deal."

"I take it you go away a lot," Lloyd commented.

Emily issued a small shrug. "A couple of weeks a year. I can't go more often because Tom and Sally—our assistant at the veterinary hospital—can't handle everything by themselves. I'll take a week here, a long weekend there. Visits to my folks, or to my brothers. Last winter I spent a week in the Bahamas, but usually my vacations aren't so exotic. Still, getting away from work for a few days is important," she added meaningfully.

Lloyd weighed her words, considering his response. "How many brothers have you got?" he asked.

She chuckled inwardly at his stubborn refusal to react to her comment about getting away from one's work. He really must be a workaholic, she decided. "Two," she answered. "They're both younger than me. Lee lives in Minneapolis—he works at a bank there. Jeff's still in college, but he'll put up with a weekend visit from his big sister once or twice a year. How about you? Any siblings?"

"No," he replied so dryly Emily couldn't help discerning that he was dissatisfied about being an only child.

"I'll tell you what," Emily said brightly, eager to cheer him up. "Let's take the boat out."

49

"The boat?"

"We can take a spin around the lake. It's early." She stood. "I've got an old canoe. Are you game?"

He contemplated her suggestion, then drank the last of his lemonade and got to his feet. "All right."

She carried their empty glasses into the kitchen, then rejoined Lloyd outside. Gus was still contentedly dozing, and she double-checked his leash to make sure it was securely tied before heading for the garage, Lloyd following her. She stored her canoe, an aluminum craft she'd bought secondhand last summer, on one side of the garage, the two scratched wooden paddles hanging by their handles on the wall above. Lloyd dragged the boat outside, then gripped its edges and hoisted it over his head with a powerful swing. Toting the paddles, Emily led him across the street and down to the dock.

She helped Lloyd lower the boat into the water and then stepped into it. He climbed in behind her. "I take it you want the stern?" she asked.

"That's the harder seat to paddle, isn't it?"

His assumption that she'd want the easier bow seat tickled her. Even after seeing her ply her carpentry skills, he still behaved like a protective male. She didn't mind. She didn't have to prove her strength to him.

They settled onto their seats and shoved away from the dock, propelling the boat out into the lake's silver center. Many other boats shared the lake with them, powerboats and catamarans and colorful Sunfishes celebrating a beautiful afternoon. Emily hoped to learn to sail someday, but for now her canoe was all she could afford, and since she could paddle it solo, she was glad to have it.

"It's lovely, isn't it?" Emily called over her shoulder, in reference to both the lake and the balmy afternoon.

"Yes." Lloyd stroked evenly through the water. When Emily permitted herself another glance backward, she noticed the tapering length of his fingers curled over the handle of his paddle, and the width of his chest. The collar of his shirt was unbuttoned, and she saw several curls of black hair peeking through the open slit of the shirt's neckline. She wished he had taken the front seat so she could see him better, but then she would have seen only his back.

His uncommon handsomeness stirred her. She recalled last night's kiss, the way the touch of Lloyd's mouth had awakened responses so deeply buried she hadn't known of their existence. Thinking about his affect on her frightened her, and she kept her eyes fastened to the calm water as their boat cut through it, heading toward the opposite shoreline.

"Did you go boating here when you visited five years ago?" she asked, hoping to silence her memories by starting a casual conversation. Yet as soon as she voiced the question she realized that it wasn't casual. When he'd visited five years ago, he'd been with his wife.

The silence that greeted her inquiry unnerved her, and she twisted in her seat to confront him. "I don't want to talk about it," he muttered, his eyes freezing her.

"All I asked was—"

"Yes, we went boating," he snapped, then directed his gaze past her. "End of discussion."

Emily reluctantly faced forward again, debating the wisdom of satisfying her curiosity. Why be wise? she decided. Lloyd would be gone tomorrow. What did she have to lose? "Your wife didn't like boats?" she pressed him.

"I said I don't want to talk about it," he growled, a barely veiled threat coloring his tone.

"I don't scare easily," she shot back.

He lapsed into silence, his eyes burning through her shirt. She could feel them on her, lacerating her with their fury. All right, so she was nosy. It wasn't as if she were insulting him. She only wanted to get to know him better. She wanted to come to terms with the sort of man who could kiss her so . . . compellingly. Was that a crime?

"When did she die?" she asked.

Lloyd refused to answer.

"Recently?"

He exhaled. "Five years ago."

"Right after your trip here?" She was correct in guessing that his lack of vacations related to his wife's death. She swallowed and made herself ask, "How did she die?"

"That's enough, Emily." His voice was quiet yet iron-hard, and Emily backed down. She wished there was some way she could show him that her interest in him was a compassionate one, that she liked him and wanted to help him—that she yearned to ease his pain. Smiling ironically, she recalled some of the people she'd known in southern California, who'd as soon tell her their life story as say hello. Utter strangers at cocktail parties would corner her and discuss their analysis, boast about their perversions, shed crocodile tears over their failed relationships. How different they were from Lloyd, whose reticence only whetted Emily's curiosity about him, whose pain, she suspected, had never been expressed in tears.

They paddled in a broad oval to one end of the lake and then back again, smoothly approaching her dock. Lloyd chivalrously disembarked first and held the boat motionless for Emily. The last half of their excursion, traveled without a word exchanged between them, had evidently calmed Lloyd, and he smiled hesitantly as he steadied Emily's footing with a hand on her shoulder. She considered apologizing for prying, but decided against it. He seemed to have cheered up.

Together, they lugged the canoe back to the garage, setting it down along the wall. Emily's eyes took a moment to adjust to the interior darkness after the glaring sunshine. She took Lloyd's paddle and hung it with her own on the nails she'd hammered into the garage wall above the canoe.

She wasn't aware of how close to her Lloyd was until she turned around. His chest was hardly an inch from hers, and his hands came to rest against the wall on either side of her head. She felt his warm, dry breath across her cheeks and realized at once that he intended to kiss her.

She wasn't prepared for it. She hadn't worked through what had happened to her the previous night when he'd kissed her. Except that she knew kissing him was dangerous. She hastily averted her face and whispered, "Lloyd—"

He lowered his head, capturing her lips with his. And then there was no escape, no escape from his mouth, no escape from the strange surge of heat it elicited within her. She leaned weakly against the wall and he pressed his body to hers, sliding his hands to her hair and running them across the skin of her neck beneath the ponytail. "Emily," he sighed. "Emily. I want you."

She wouldn't have been able to speak even if she'd known what to say. Her only vaguely coherent thought was that she wanted him too, but her desire was totally out of line. That she should want *any* man, let alone a man she hardly knew, was a completely alien experience to her.

He nipped at her trembling lower lip, then ran his tongue along her teeth, coaxing them apart. His tongue delved deep into her mouth, seeking its partner. When he discovered it she felt herself melting, her organs liquefying in the fire building inside her, radiating from the pit of her stomach outward in all directions. His hands brushed through her hair to her shoulders, forward to her collarbones. "Lloyd . . ." Her breath was shaky, her knees threatening to buckle.

"I can't stop thinking about you," he whispered.

"First last night and then this morning, seeing you while you worked. . . ." His mouth traveled over her face, grazing her forehead, her temple, her closed eyelids. "You're so strong, Emily, so incredibly strong. . . ."

One of his hands dropped to her breast, his long fingers caressing the soft flesh. He traced the full curve of it, then slid forward to tantalize the budding nipple at its center. She groaned as an erotic flame spread from her breast down to her pelvis. Instinctively she angled herself against him, and was aware of his arousal.

"No," she said, "no, I can't," as if speaking the words would make them true. Yet her hips spoke a truth all their own, moving against his, savoring his obvious response.

His other hand wandered to her waist, bare where she had tied her blouse. He explored the satiny skin exposed there, his fingers stroking her with gentle insistence. Then he let his hand drop to the curve of her bottom, holding her tightly to himself. She groaned again, awash in sensations frightening in their power and unfamiliarity. "Why not?" he demanded softly before touching his lips to hers again. "Why not?"

She tore her face from his and spun away, clinging to the wall and praying it would keep her from collapsing. "What do you expect from me, Lloyd?" she wailed, despising the feeble, quivering tone of her voice. "What the hell do you want?"

"I think it's obvious," he said candidly. "You want me, too, Emily. Don't deny it."

"I don't even know you."

He hovered behind her, his hands gently clasping her shoulders. "You know me enough to want me," he stated huskily. "You know me enough to set us both on fire when we kiss."

"So what?" She sounded stronger to herself, although she was acutely aware of her precarious mental balance. "So what? You're still a stranger. When I ask you anything about yourself, you run away. You hide from me."

"Hide what?"

"Your wife. My God, Lloyd, the way you react—for all I know, you killed her! Who the hell are you, anyway?"

A chill filtered down her spine, and she realized that Lloyd had recoiled from her. She dared to turn around and found him several feet away, staring at her, his face drawn into a mask of icy rage. A new kind of fear tore at her nerve endings, and without thinking she darted from the garage.

She didn't stop running until she'd reached her kitchen. She was shivering, gulping for air. She wasn't certain what she'd seen in his face, but it had shaken her much more than his kiss. She slumped onto a chair and buried her head in her hands.

"Actually, she killed herself."

She hadn't heard Lloyd entering her house, and the sudden sound of his voice made her jump. He was standing in the kitchen doorway, leaning against the doorframe, his expression typically inscrutable. But it was gentler somehow, his eyes a pensive blue, his mouth grim but not hard, as if the residue of Emily's kiss still lingered on it.

"I could use a drink," he commented.

She nodded woodenly and rose. His revelation slowly solidified in her brain: his wife had killed herself. No wonder he hadn't wanted to discuss it. If an untimely death was tragic, a suicide was even more so. She felt oddly guilty for having forced from him a fact that he clearly hadn't wanted to share with her.

"Bloody Mary, right?" she managed to ask. The interior of her mouth felt dry and sandpapery.

"Skip the 'Bloody.' "

She nodded again and filled a glass with ice and vodka for him. She chose just the "Bloody" for herself, figuring that tomato juice was as potent a beverage as she could handle. Lloyd took both drinks and carried them out to the front porch.

Gus greeted them with a howl. Obviously he was tired of being leashed, and before taking a seat beside Lloyd, Emily untied him and let him loose in the house. Then she lowered herself onto the step next to Lloyd and accepted her glass of tomato juice from him.

She took a bracing sip. "I'm sorry, Lloyd," she said falteringly. "We don't have to talk about it if you don't want."

"It's too late for that," he noted acerbically before taking a drink of his vodka.

"It—it isn't your fault," she stammered. "What happened to your wife, I mean. It's nothing to be ashamed of."

He mulled over her words, "Who says I'm ashamed?"

"Well . . . the way you acted in the canoe, as if you were trying to run away from it. I know it must be painful for you, but—"

"Are you going to psychoanalyze me?" His gruff tone convinced Emily that he was furious with her, and his anger made her ache.

"I only meant—well, it's common for the survivor to feel as if he were somehow to blame."

He cast her a sharp, flinty glance. "What do you know about it?"

"I've read a few things."

"You're an animal doctor," he scoffed. "Why don't you stick to your specialty?"

"People are animals, too," Emily pointed out. She turned her gaze to the water. The sun had begun its descent, and the trees lining the lake's shoreline cast long shadows across its silver surface. "Do you have any children?" she asked.

"No," he said curtly.

"You don't like children?" she asked at his grim tone. "I didn't say that."

She glimpsed his profile, his high forehead capped by dark, untamed curls, his long, straight nose underlined by his mustache, his angular chin jutting forward. His knees were spread apart, his forearms resting on them, his fingers curved around the glass of vodka. "I bet you put them in the same category as pets," she guessed. "They're demanding, they take a lot of time and attention, and they aren't easy to farm out when you want to go away for a couple of days."

He shot her a fierce look. "Let up, Emily, all right? You're coming at me like a battering ram."

Because I want to break down the wall, she responded silently. *Because I want to break through.* She drank her juice, disappointed by Lloyd's retreat from her. "If you want to leave, nobody's stopping you."

"I'm stopping me," he muttered, then exhaled and studied his drink. His voice was low and taut when he spoke. "I told you, Emily—I've been thinking about you. Ever since you stopped by the side of the road yesterday and went racing off in search of that deer. . ." He paused to sort his thoughts. "There's something about you. You're so. . ." He shook his head, unable to come up with the right word.

"Strong?" she supplied. That was what he'd said in the garage: she was strong. Not beautiful, not sexy, not even womanly. Strong.

He nodded. "Strong. Healthy." He turned to look at her again, this time giving her a long, searching perusal. "Brave," he concluded.

"Why? Because I wasn't afraid of that deer?"

"Because you aren't afraid of me."

But she *was* afraid of him, afraid of the way his kisses burned through her, afraid of the power his lips and hands exerted over her. She averted her gaze, unsure of what to say. Gus bailed her out by scratching the front door and whining. "I've got to feed Gus," she announced, relieved of the need to verbalize her feelings.

Lloyd downed the last of his drink and stood when Emily did. "Do you play tennis?" he inquired.

His unexpected question startled her, but she covered with a shrug. "I'm a little rusty," she confessed. She had played regularly in Los Angeles, but since moving to New Preston, she played only occasionally with Tom and his wife.

"The inn has a tennis court," he reminded her. "We could play a set tomorrow."

"Aren't you leaving tomorrow?" she asked.

"Not in the morning. We could play early, then have some breakfast together."

His invitation seemed innocent enough, but she knew there was something far from innocent in the way his eyes traveled over her upturned face, in the way her skin warmed beneath his scrutiny. "Look, Lloyd," she demurred. "I'm not . . . I'm not going to go to bed with you, if that's why you're inviting me."

Her frankness evoked a wistful smile from him. "That's not why I'm asking," he said, though he couldn't resist adding, "Any particular reason why you won't go to bed with me?"

Yes, indeed, she muttered beneath her breath. A very particular reason. She didn't function well in bed. Lloyd thought she was strong and healthy, and she'd just as soon let him continue to think of her that way. That they were attracted to each other was irrelevant. She wasn't going to set herself up for failure with him. "It wouldn't be a good idea, that's all," she replied, deciding that was a fairly honest answer.

He measured her words. Then his smile broadened slightly. "Tennis and breakfast. How about it?"

Tennis and breakfast and then he would be gone. Why not? she thought. She'd gotten him to open up a little today. Maybe she could get him to open a little more tomorrow. Then he could return home to Hartford, to his apartment and his economic forecasting firm and remember with fondness—she hoped!—the brave woman who had dared to come at him like a battering ram. Maybe his eyes would remain the gentle pale blue they were now, instead of changing to that brutal icy silver, and he'd appreciate what she'd done for him.

And as for herself . . . as for herself, she wanted to spend more time with him, even if only a couple of hours tomorrow morning. She wasn't yet ready to say good-bye to him. "Tennis and breakfast," she accepted. "You're on."

"Do you want me to pick you up?" he asked.

"No, I can drive over. I know the place."

Gus whined again. Emily heard his claws scratching the lower panels of the door. "Eight o'clock," Lloyd said. "Before it gets too hot to play."

"Eight o'clock." She bent to pick up their glasses. "I'll see you then."

He waited until she'd straightened up, then touched his mouth to hers. Even his light, gentlemanly kiss of farewell affected her, igniting tiny sparks that rippled through her. She felt a blush rise to her cheeks. "Good-bye, Lloyd," she mumbled, oddly embarrassed by her response to him.

He watched her turn and enter the house, then loped down the sturdy new porch steps to his car.

4

The raucous night song of crickets and bullfrogs wafted through Emily's open windows, filling her living room with a shrill cacophony. She switched on the television set and dropped onto her plump, tweedy couch, seeking distraction.

She hadn't been able to eat dinner. She ought to have been hungry, given the day's activity and her failure to eat lunch. But the light meal of soup and salad she'd prepared for herself had done nothing to awaken her appetite, and she'd ended up throwing it away.

Gus prowled the cozy living room, padding to the plank-and-cinder-block bookcases along one wall, to the easy chair across from the sofa, to the wood stove, then to the rug at Emily's feet. She ran her bare foot along his belly and he yawned contentedly.

Lloyd. Lloyd Gordon. His name ran through Emily's head, his face, his body. His mesmerizing eyes. Discovering what was behind the pain she read in them hadn't slaked her curiosity as she had thought it would. It only made her want to know him better.

His eyes reminded her of an Alaskan malamute's, clear and blue and unspeakably lovely. Lloyd wasn't a dog, but he was an animal. All human beings were. Their superior intelligence gave them the means to hide their pain more easily than the lower orders of animals could, but their eyes always gave them away. That Emily had been able to discover the cause of Lloyd's pain didn't mean she could cure him, but the discovery pleased her nonetheless.

He thought she was strong and healthy—not the most romantic of sentiments, but for the most part accurate. Except for one aspect of her body, one vital part of her that wasn't healthy at all. As she'd endeavored to unlock Lloyd's ailment, his behavior had encouraged her to unlock hers. The power of his kisses, his caresses, his whispered desire had nearly made her reveal her secret to him.

She doubted, though, that Lloyd would be successful in curing her. Years of disappointment with Ed indicated to Emily that hers was a condition without a cure.

"Look, Gus," she murmured with a nod toward the television screen. "It's Eddie's show." Gus had never known Ed; Emily had adopted the scraggly mongrel pup from the county's SPCA a few months after moving to New Preston. But she'd told Gus a great deal about her former husband, and the dog turned his brown-eyed gaze to the television screen.

Because Emily didn't regularly watch Ed's show, she had no idea what was going on in the current episode. Her attention focused on her ex-husband, who portrayed the callow son of an oil magnate in the series. He was still awfully good-looking, she acknowledged, his light brown hair shorter than it had been during their years together, the laugh lines framing his eyes showing

61

signs of permanence. She recalled Ed's performance in the Syracuse theater's production of *Romeo and Juliet* and decided that he was wasting his talent in the television show.

The scene's dialogue conveyed the fact that he was involved in an extramarital affair with the daughter of his father's rival. "How appropriate," Emily sniffed as she watched a gorgeous young actress peel Ed's shirt from his shoulders. Emily tried to remember what she had felt when Ed used to kiss her. Something—she must have felt something. Yes, she had: a rise of warmth in her flesh, an expectant tensing in her muscles. The kisses had been fine, the preliminaries had excited her. But they'd led to nothing. Nothing but frustration and anguish. Ed was a sexy, talented man, no less so than Lloyd. That she had desired Lloyd that afternoon was irrelevant. There was no point in believing that if she'd satisfied her desire she would have enjoyed the experience any more than she'd ever enjoyed sex with Ed.

Gus stirred and roved restlessly to the door. He sniffed at it, then scratched and whimpered. Emily crossed the room and inched open the door. "Nobody out there," she informed Gus as she closed the door. But he remained unconvinced, pacing in a circle before the door and whining, sensing something Emily couldn't fathom. Maybe a dog in heat was somewhere nearby. Gus was in the throes of puberty; perhaps he was lusting for a willing sweetheart. "Forget it, pal," she scolded him sternly. "Try to be civilized—keep your instincts in check. Give the poor bitch a break." She returned to the couch, hoping Gus would follow, but he remained by the door, growling softly. When Ed's show ended, Emily turned off the set and retired to her bedroom. But Gus stayed resolutely at the door, whimpering and pacing long into the night.

Emily arose at seven-thirty and donned a short yellow tennis dress with white trim, a pair of low-cut sneaker socks, and her sneakers. She hadn't worn the tennis dress since leaving Los Angeles. When she played tennis with Tom and his wife in Litchfield, she usually dressed in shorts and a T-shirt. Tom didn't impose a dress code on his backyard concrete court, and she didn't have to impress him the way Ed had compelled her to impress his colleagues in Hollywood with regulation chic apparel.

She brushed her hair into a ponytail, gathered her racket and a towel, and then roused Gus from sleep. After filling a water dish for him and pulling several dog biscuits from a box beneath the sink, she led him outside and tied him to his runner leash. "I'll be back later," she promised him. "Stay out of trouble."

She ambled around the house to her station wagon and climbed in. The morning resembled the previous day in its sunny mildness, and anticipating seeing Lloyd cheered her. She'd made things pretty clear to him yesterday, and she didn't think he'd push things. He was reserved by nature, his fiery kisses notwithstanding. Tennis and breakfast was what they'd agreed to, and she was certain he'd stick to that agenda.

She arrived promptly at the inn and parked in the lot beside the sprawling white clapboard building. Entering the antique-filled parlor, she crossed to the desk and asked the clerk to call Lloyd.

Before the clerk could respond, Emily heard footsteps on the carpeted stairway to her left, and Lloyd descended into view. He wore a short-sleeved knit shirt and matching shorts, their crisp snow-white setting off his bronze complexion. Like her, he carried a tennis racket and a towel, as well as a can of tennis balls. His clear eyes wandered down Emily's body, taking in her wide shoulders and her strong upper arms, her sleek, muscular thighs and firm calves. Something in his measuring gaze made her feel acutely exposed.

Swallowing the tremor of nervousness in her throat,

she lifted her eyes to his face. His mouth spread in a warm, genuine smile that stilled her anxiety. "Good morning," he greeted her.

"Good morning," she replied before allowing him to escort her from the building.

They followed a slate path to the tennis court, which was vacant. Emily was no longer accustomed to playing on clay, and the spongy surface of the court delighted her. Lloyd considerately gave her the advantage of the shaded side, strolling around the net to face the sun, and he tossed her two balls. "You can serve first," he invited her.

She did. Her serve was clean and legal, though not terribly dynamic. Lloyd had no difficulty returning it. They began a relaxed rally, Emily warming to the game as she sized up her opponent. Lloyd's arms were long and sinewy, yet he seemed to check himself, deliberately limiting the power of his swing. It occurred to her that he was holding back, allowing her to win, and she resented it.

When she won the first game in six serves, she threw him the balls and grumbled, "You don't have to play down to me, you know."

"What do you mean?" he protested.

"You're going easy on me. Come on, Lloyd—show me what you've got. I can take it."

He threw back his head and issued a deep chuckle. "Sorry, Billie Jean," he teased. "I'll give it my all."

That she'd gotten him to laugh and apologize simultaneously pleased her enormously, and she felt her cheeks dimpling as she bounced expectantly on her toes and awaited his serve.

It rocketed past her, careening off the clay at an unexpected angle. Lloyd clearly could put a devastating spin on the ball, she admitted as she sucked in her breath and announced, "Okay, Ace, now I'm *really* ready."

He laughed again, then served. This time she *was* ready, positioning herself to attack the ricocheting ball, and the pace of the game accelerated. After Lloyd's third serve she rushed the net, strategically placing the ball in his half of the court several times, although he finally succeeded in lobbing it past her.

He was playing at full force, and so was Emily. She recognized that he was a better player than she, but she didn't care. She enjoyed the challenge of the game. She'd much rather lose fairly than win through Lloyd's coddling of her.

They played for nearly an hour, the set concluding in a score of six to four. Emily approached the net, and Lloyd offered a polite handshake above it. "Aren't you going to leap over the net?" she taunted him.

He was perspiring as much as Emily, slightly out of breath. "Who has the strength?" he complained amiably. "You put me through my paces. You didn't learn to play like that in Kansas, did you?"

Emily chuckled. "Do I detect some of that stodgy Eastern provincialism?" she chided him.

Noticing another couple waiting for the court, they gathered their things and moved from the court onto the adjacent grass. "Seriously," Lloyd pressed her. "Do people play tennis in Kansas?"

She couldn't resist ribbing him. "Indeed they do," she deadpanned. "We got tennis in around nineteen-seventy, right after indoor plumbing and electricity."

He accepted her kidding with a grudging smile. "Hungry?" he asked as he ran his towel over his face.

"Starving." After not having bothered to eat all day yesterday, Emily felt her appetite returning in full force.

Lloyd guided her toward the inn's main building. "We could freshen up in my room before breakfast if you'd like," he offered.

She looked at him askance, then shook her head. Merely the light clasp of his hand on her elbow reminded her of the way she had felt in his arms, and she didn't trust herself—or him—to go to his room. "Haven't they got a bathroom near the dining room?"

He evidently discerned her suspicion, and he acknowledged it with a wry nod. They entered the building and he pointed out the ladies' room to her. "I'll meet you in the dining room," he said as he vanished into the men's room.

Emily entered the powder room and moved directly to one of the sinks, where she washed her damp, flushed face. She pulled her hairbrush from her purse and removed the barrette that had held her hair in its ponytail. She brushed it loose, the heavy golden locks glimmering in the light of the fixture above the mirror.

Leaving the bathroom, she found Lloyd loitering by the dining room's entrance, watching for her. As soon as she joined him, he requested an outdoor table from the hostess, who led them to a canopied terrace overlooking the tennis court and, beyond it, the lake. The summery blue sky was reflected in its tranquil surface. A magnificent blue, Emily opined. Like the blue of Lloyd's eyes. They, too, were warm and summery, sparkling with pleasure. Not a trace of ice in them, she mused happily.

"We have a brunch buffet today," the hostess informed them. "Please help yourselves. I'll have someone bring you coffee."

Once the hostess had gone, Lloyd and Emily set their rackets and towels on an empty chair, then returned to the dining room to select their meals. A chef stood at one end of the room preparing omelets. "I'll get some eggs for you," said Lloyd. "Go check out the buffet."

Emily lifted a plate and ambled along the groaning board, which featured casserole dishes containing chicken à la king, French toast, waffles, and fresh fruit salad. An adjacent table was laden with Danish pastries, blueberry muffins, and croissants. Emily loaded her plate until there was no room left on it. She was truly ravenous, and everything looked too appetizing to pass up. She couldn't resist taking at least a small taste of each dish.

She returned to their outdoor table, and Lloyd soon arrived, carrying a plate with two omelets on it as well as a platter of samplings from the buffet. He studied Emily's heaping plate and grinned. "Are you really going to eat all that?"

"I'll go on a diet tomorrow," she replied with a shrug, too hungry to feel self-conscious.

He sat and passed her an omelet, his smile expanding. "Don't," he declared. "I like a woman with a healthy appetite."

Emily realized that she could take that comment in more ways than one, but she refused to let it rattle her. She tasted her omelet. "This is delicious," she announced.

Lloyd dug into his own food. "Tell me more about Kansas," he requested. "Did you really become a tennis whiz there?"

She shook her head. "The regional high school had courts, so I learned the rudiments there. But I didn't get good at it until college."

"Cornell," he recalled. "That's a pretty decent school for a midwestern farm girl."

"There aren't that many veterinary programs in the country," Emily explained. "Cornell has one of the best. And I'm not a farm girl. I grew up in town."

"Town," he scoffed. "How big was this town?"

"Population three hundred seventy, according to the latest census," Emily confirmed. "It's shrunk since I lived there. My generation isn't sticking around. Farming's too risky a venture these days, at least family farming."

"But you weren't a farm girl," Lloyd echoed. "Were you the rich kid in town?"

Emily laughed. "My parents own a hardware store carrying mostly farm supplies, which means that if the farmers are doing poorly, so are my folks. Everyone buys on credit, and if their crop doesn't come in they can't pay. But you can't very well dun your friends and neighbors. Everyone's too dependent on each other. So no, we weren't any richer than the farmers."

"Hardware store, huh?"

"Also the town's movie theater," Emily related with a chuckle. "The building had a big white exterior wall of stucco, with a grassy field beside it. So once a week during fair weather, my father would rent a film and show it on the wall. He doesn't do that anymore, though. Everybody's got satellite dishes; they can pick up the movie channels on their television sets at home."

Lloyd ate in silent thought for several minutes, then lifted his twinkling eyes to Emily. "You seem more the Kansas type than the Hollywood type," he stated.

"Oh? What's the Kansas type, Mr. Eastern Provincial?"

He laughed and leaned back to appraise her. "When I was growing up in Manhattan, I had a vision of Kansas as a place filled with nubile blond girls losing their virginity in haylofts at the age of fourteen."

Emily nearly choked on her coffee. "What?!" she objected with a guffaw.

Lloyd seemed disappointed. "No haylofts?"

Emily took another sip of coffee to calm her hysterical giggling. "Oh sure, we had haylofts. And corncribs. But Lloyd—fourteen? Good God, at fourteen I thought French kissing was the ultimate sin."

"Another myth shattered," Lloyd murmured with feigned sadness.

"Honestly!" She was still shaking with laughter. "A girl would have been crazy to mess around with a local boy. We all knew each other too well. We all grew up together, skinny-dipped together, raised Four-H animals together. It would be like incest, fooling around with one of the guys." She smiled sheepishly. "Well, a little fooling around, maybe, but nothing serious."

"In haylofts?"

"I hate to destroy your myths, Lloyd, but haylofts aren't particularly romantic. Especially if you've got livestock below. They smell of animal droppings. Corncribs are a little better, but spend more than a minute in one and you're covered with corn dust. I assure you, Manhattan is much more conducive to romance than Kansas."

"Have you been to Manhattan?"

"A few times. My ex-husband was from Long Island," she reminded him. "We'd go to the city when we were visiting his parents."

"And you think it's a romantic place?"

"Well . . ." Emily drained her coffee cup and relaxed in her chair, her eyes scanning the panorama beyond the terrace. "It's too crowded for me, and it's polluted. But I liked going to the shows, and the museums. Central Park was nice." She turned back to Lloyd. "What did fourteen-year-old girls do in Manhattan?"

"Nothing," he answered glumly, then grinned. "I didn't get to meet too many of them. I attended an all-boys' prep school. What little I knew about fourteen-year-old girls came from subjecting myself to inter-school dances, which were unbelievably boring. My friends and I learned the facts of life by reading *Playboy*." When Emily curled her lip in disdain, Lloyd laughed.

"How'd you wind up in Connecticut?" she asked.

"Yale," he informed her. "I took both my undergraduate and graduate degrees there. And then the government hired me as a researcher, and I decided to stay."

"How long did you work for the government?"

His smile faded, his eyes cooling slightly. "Four years."

"You didn't enjoy it?"

He shook his head. "It was stifling."

"Why did you stick with it for four years?" Emily pried. At Lloyd's lengthening silence, she dared to ask, "Your wife?"

"My wife," he confirmed tersely. He was withdrawing again, and Emily struggled to think of a way to recapture the closeness they'd seemed to feel earlier. But before she could come up with anything, his face brightened. "You didn't bring a bathing suit with you by any chance, did you?"

"You want to go swimming?" The late morning was already quite warm, and she spotted a few bathers by the water's edge. Lloyd nodded, and she said, "I could drive back home for one."

"Why don't we . . ." He stared toward the water for a moment, then turned back to her. "Why don't we take one of the inn's boats and row back to your place?"

The idea struck Emily as unexpectedly whimsical, and she instantly warmed to it. "Okay, let's."

Lloyd flagged down the waitress, who presented a check for him to sign. Then they collected their tennis gear and entered the building. Emily waited for Lloyd at the foot of the stairs while he went to his room to leave his racket. When he returned several minutes later, he was wearing dark blue swimming briefs and an unbuttoned oxford shirt.

Emily watched him descend the stairs, transfixed by the sight of his splendid physique. His chest was muscular without being muscle-bound, and an enticing triangle of black hair adorned the rippling stretch of coppery skin. His long legs were also covered by a fine webbing of black hair. She felt as if she were glued to the parlor floor, gawking at the extraordinary specimen of manhood Lloyd presented.

If her uncharacteristic ogling annoyed him, he didn't

show it. He seemed rather amused as he took Emily's racket and then held the door open for her.

They strolled down the slope to the waterfront. The inn's canoe had already been taken by another guest, an employee told them, but they were welcome to take the rowboat. Lloyd handed Emily's racket to her, freeing his hands to carry the oars to the boat. He slid them into their locks and gestured Emily toward the bow seat.

She dropped her racket into the boat, then hesitated. Perhaps it was only Lloyd's imposing virility that caused her defenses to rise, but she wasn't going to let him be manly and chivalrous. "I'll row," she announced.

"What?"

"I'll row. You can ride."

He studied her for several long seconds, trying to make sense of her offer. "We'll both row," he resolved, helping her onto the oarsman's seat.

He shoved the boat into the water, then climbed in, his wet feet splattering Emily's ankles. She slid over on the bench to make room for him, and together they plied the oars through the water.

Lloyd's stroke was stronger than hers, and the boat hooked in a circle. It took them a couple of minutes to coordinate, their elbows and hips bumping as they tried to find a compatible rhythm. At last the boat righted itself and headed directly to the center of the lake.

They didn't speak, but Emily felt undeniably close to Lloyd. Rowing with him struck her as strangely intimate, a way of sharing unlike any other. She forgot about his abrupt cooling when she'd mentioned his wife at breakfast. Everything about him seemed warm now, his shoulder lightly brushing hers, his hands matching hers as they gripped the oar handles, his lips curved in a gentle smile. Rowing *with* him was far more satisfying than merely rowing him would have been.

Within fifteen minutes they arrived at her boat dock.

They glided beyond it to the pebbly beach and, to protect Emily's sneakers, Lloyd leaped out and pushed the boat onto dry land. "You know, it's much more private here," she remarked as she scanned the empty shoreline. "We could swim here instead of at the inn."

He considered her suggestion and grinned. "It's so private we could swim naked," he noted. At her glower, he justified himself: "You said you used to skinny-dip in Kansas."

"When I was eight years old," she emphasized. "There's a big difference between skinny-dipping when you're eight and when you're twenty-nine."

Lloyd nodded, offering a sly grin. "There certainly is. If you were eight, I wouldn't be at all interested in swimming naked with you." He relented with a laugh. "Go put on a bathing suit. I'll wait for you here."

"I'll be right back," she said as she scooped up her racket and jogged across the street to her house.

In her bedroom, she rummaged through her bureau until she found her swimsuit, a slim-fitting maillot of bright red. She pulled it on and studied herself in the mirror. The string-thin straps emphasized the width of her shoulders, and the clinging red material called attention to the lush curves of her breasts and hips. She grimaced as a bitter picture flashed through her mind, an image of a slender, dark actress, Ed's first Hollywood fling. Emily had met her by the pool of their tennis club, and Ed had introduced her as a guest artist on his series. She'd been wearing a skimpy white bikini. She couldn't have weighed more than a hundred pounds; her body had practically disappeared when she turned sideways. As soon as Ed had vanished to talk shop with another colleague at the poolside bar, the woman had cheerfully informed Emily that she found Ed to be excellent in bed. Nobody in that crowd hid anything, not even their adulteries.

Emily rarely thought about the woman, but her own

reflection in the mirror reminded her of the way her sturdy figure compared with the sylphlike women who caught Ed's fancy. "Ten pounds," Emily muttered as she sucked in her stomach. No, ten pounds wouldn't make much difference. She would always look well-fed and robust.

Sighing, she paused in the hall to pull two towels from her linen closet. Then she entered the kitchen and strode to the window to check on Gus. He was yanking at his runner leash, straining toward the forest and baying softly. There must be a bitch in heat somewhere, Emily mused. Maybe she could distract Gus by bringing him with her to the waterfront.

She left the house through the kitchen door, and Gus raced toward her, thrilled to see her. As soon as she unfastened his rope from the runner, he jerked toward the woods again. "No way, buster," she snapped. "You're coming with me." She dragged the dog around the house, and he reluctantly fell into step beside her.

When Lloyd saw Gus he scowled. "What's he doing here?" he asked accusingly as Emily tied Gus's rope around a young sycamore tree that had sprouted near the shore.

"Keeping us company," Emily answered. She tossed the towels onto the dock, then stalked past Lloyd to the dock's end and hurled herself into the lake in a graceless cannonball.

The water was frigid, and she swallowed the urge to shriek as she bobbed to the surface. Lloyd had shed his shirt and was standing on the edge of the dock, watching her. "How is it?" he asked.

"Wonderful," she lied.

He nodded, then executed a perfect racing dive off the end of the dock. Surfacing, he issued a furious roar. "It's freezing, Emily!" he sputtered as he treaded water and slicked his hair back from his face. "Why did you tell me it was wonderful?"

"You wouldn't have come in otherwise," she pointed out.

"Hmm." He conceded with a nod. "Well, we'd better keep moving to warm up." He surveyed the shoreline, spotting another boat dock eighty yards away. "I'll race you to that dock," he challenged her.

"Forget it," Emily declined. "Isn't beating me at tennis enough for your ego?"

"You're a bad swimmer?" he asked.

"Just a slow one," she told him, illustrating the point by moving in a leisurely freestyle away from the dock.

Lloyd accompanied her, using a sidestroke so he could watch her. "You swim well," he observed.

"So do you. You're pretty athletic for a city kid."

"Now who's being provincial?" he mocked her. "Believe it or not, we do have tennis courts and swimming pools in New York City."

Gus was barking at a squirrel, and when Emily glanced toward him she realized that they'd traveled far from the shore. She rolled onto her back and swam a relaxed backstroke toward the beach, Lloyd adjusting his pace to hers. Several yards from shore he stopped and gazed at the dog. "He's all right," he said.

Emily stopped as well. "He's probably much better off than we are. Warmer, anyway."

"I'm pretty warm," Lloyd commented softly. "Getting warmer every minute."

Emily's eyes met his. She had no difficulty reading the intention in them, and she tried to think of something to say that might prevent Lloyd from kissing her. But the words wouldn't come. Her heart blocked her mind, its rapid beating insisting that she wanted Lloyd's kiss more than she feared it.

He hesitated, as if to give her the opportunity to speak, to stop him. He apparently took her silence as permission. Moving in a smooth arc through the water, his arm closed around her shoulders, pulling her to him. His mouth crushed softly against hers, and his other arm looped about her back, pressing her to his chest. Emily gasped at Lloyd's sudden rekindling of the fire within her, and at the parting of her lips, his tongue darted inside.

She could no more keep him from kissing her than she could keep herself from responding. Her hands reached for his head, grasping the thick, damp tendrils that covered his scalp, and her tongue matched his in its fervor. Her breasts pressed against the tight fabric of her swimsuit, her nipples hardening as they brushed against his chest.

He slid his hands down to her hips, easing her legs up to circle his torso. Then he gripped her waist. She felt light in his embrace; whether it was her body's natural buoyancy in the water or the length of his fingers fanning around her sides, she felt small and dainty in his arms.

"Emily," he whispered, catching her lower lip in his teeth. "Emily." His fingers stroked across her naked back to the lower edge of her swimsuit. They slid beneath the fabric, exploring the soft flesh of her bottom. Sensing the electric shiver that tore through her, he groaned.

She clung to him, her arms snug around his neck, her mouth moving hungrily over his mustache, down to his jaw, his neck, his shoulder. "Emily," he whispered into her hair. "Let's make love."

"No."

Even as she spoke the word her body was defying her, one hand clinging tightly to his neck while the other toured the ridge of his shoulder, combing down through the matted hair of his chest to caress his ribs. She tried to will herself to regain her control. She knew she was arousing him; she knew what she was doing wasn't fair to him. Nor to herself. She was excited now, transported, aroused beyond belief. But it would lead nowhere, she reminded herself. She should stop; there was no point in encouraging this.

Her legs unclenched, sliding along his as her feet searched for the lake's bottom. The friction of her smooth thighs against his lightly haired skin caused her to shiver again. "No," she murmured as much to herself as to him.

He lifted one hand to her hair, running it through the wet sheet of gold that draped her shoulders. "Why not?"

"It just . . ." She swallowed and closed her eyes, unable to look at him. "It won't work, that's all."

"Something about me?" he asked.

She shook her head. "Something about me," she breathed.

He ruminated for a minute, then urged her head against his shoulder, his fingers still stroking her hair. "You want to talk about it?"

"No."

"I thought your life was an open book."

"Not that page," she whispered raggedly.

He seemed to be considering whether to question her further, then chose not to. She was relieved by his decision not to probe, not to force from her the painful admission that, as much as she responded to him now, she would fail disastrously if they made love. She was relieved, but also abashed. She'd been a busybody with him, after all, and he'd finally opened up to her—a little, anyway. But this was one thing she couldn't reveal. It was the last thing in the world she could reveal to him.

"Do you want me to leave?" he asked.

No, she thought, *no, I want you to stay forever, just stay here and hold me.* What she felt in his arms transcended anything she'd ever felt before. That was enough for her, more than enough. But it wasn't enough for Lloyd. It couldn't be. He was a man, after all, a strong, sensual man. He obviously wanted more than Emily was capable of giving.

"Emily?"

"You probably have to leave for Hartford soon anyway," she mumbled.

He exhaled, then nodded. He kept one arm around her as they walked back to the shore. Gus eyed them and seemed to smile, scampering toward them. "I've got to pick up my car," she noted dully.

"Why don't you go throw some dry clothes on, and then we'll row back to the inn?" Lloyd suggested.

His voice was muted, gentle. If he was disappointed, he didn't show it. Emily longed to fling her arms around him, to kiss him, to thank him for not hating her. But to do that would send him the wrong signal, so she only gave him a feeble smile and walked on wobbly legs to her house.

She shrugged into a terry-cloth beach jacket, ran a brush through her hair, and grabbed her purse. Then she left the house and started back toward the lake.

At the road she stopped. Lloyd had his back to her. He'd donned his shirt and wrapped one of the towels around his neck. Gus sat patiently beside him, nuzzling his hand.

Lloyd was stroking Gus. Scratching Gus's nose, ruffling his fingers between Gus's ears, massaging the thick, dark fur along Gus's throat. Lloyd's eyes were fixed on the lake, but his hand remained on Gus. Gus craned his neck to afford Lloyd access to all the places where he favored scratching, and Lloyd wordlessly obliged. Gus's eyes glowed. His tongue hung happily out of the side of his mouth, and he issued small grunts of contentment.

For a long time Emily didn't dare to move. One

77

abrupt motion might frighten Lloyd. She recalled her concern about scaring the deer two days earlier. It was the same concern she felt now, a concern about disturbing a precious moment, a private communion.

So she didn't approach. She simply watched. She watched until Lloyd let his hand drop from Gus's head and turned impatiently toward the house. "Here I am," she said, smiling sheepishly and hurrying toward the water.

Neither of them spoke as they traveled back to the inn. Lloyd rowed; Emily didn't bother arguing with him about it. She sat facing him, but his face was lost in shadow and when she caught glimpses of his eyes they seemed impassive.

She hadn't really, seriously considered his suggestion that they make love, had she? She couldn't have. As attractive as he was, he was still a stranger to her, only a tourist passing through. As she watched the grim line of his mouth, his lips pressed together in concentration, and the strain of his arms and shoulders as he maneuvered the oars, she reminded herself that for all the time they'd spent together over the past two days, she hardly knew him. He'd be gone soon and she'd never see him again. Of course Emily hadn't given serious thought to making love with him.

Yes, she had. She'd thought about it the moment he'd kissed her Friday night. She'd thought about it yesterday in her garage. And today at the lake. And plenty of moments in between, even when he wasn't with her. She was astonished by the realization, and more than a little horrified. How could she have let herself be swept away by a total stranger?

Well, she *hadn't* been swept away. She'd come close, but she'd held him off. What astonished her, she admitted, was the fact that it wasn't her sense of propriety that had convinced her to hold him off but merely her knowledge of her own shortcomings, her awareness that their lovemaking would only leave her aching with disappointment.

She studied the water, tracing with her eyes the circular eddies that followed in the wake of the oars' strokes. She was shocked by her rashness, by her lack of caution with Lloyd. It wasn't like her at all. She was amost glad that he'd be leaving, giving her the opportunity to recover her common sense.

Lloyd steered the boat smoothly onto the beach and helped her out. He continued to hold her hand as they climbed the incline toward the parking lot. He walked her to her car and leaned against its roof as she fidgeted with the keys. When she unlocked the door and swung it open he took her arm, preventing her from getting in. "I'd like to see you again," he said.

"What?" Her dark eyes widened as she turned to him.

"I'd like to see you again," he repeated.

She wasn't sure why he would. "You don't—you don't have to say that," she stammered, assuming he was just trying to be polite.

"I know I don't," Lloyd agreed dryly, reminding Emily that he wasn't the sort of man who did things out of courtesy. "Can I have your phone number?"

"Of course," she said hastily, and Lloyd smiled. He released her arm so she could lean across the front seat to reach the glove compartment. She located a notepad and pen inside, and jotted her telephone number down for Lloyd. "Hartford's a long way to travel to pick up a date," she pointed out.

"Not that long," he countered lightly as he folded the scrap of paper and stuffed it into his shirt pocket. "Who knows? Maybe I'll want to take another vacation here at the lake before five years elapse."

She couldn't help grinning. "It wouldn't hurt, Lloyd," she teased.

She settled herself behind the wheel and turned on

the engine. Lloyd bent over and grazed her lips with his. "I'll call you," he whispered before shutting the door and stepping out of her way. She eased out of the parking space and pointed her car toward the road. Checking her rearview mirror, she saw Lloyd still standing in the parking lot, watching her until she had driven away.

5

He called Monday night. "I'd like to see you this weekend," he declared.

Leaning against her kitchen counter, Emily was only half aware of Gus's roaming and growling. He slouched from the kitchen door to the front door and back again, anxious to go outside. When she'd arrived home from the animal hospital earlier that evening, she'd found him stretching his runner leash to the breaking point. She'd have to buy a thicker tether for him tomorrow, she resolved, or some receptive lady dog was going to get an unwelcome visitor.

But her concern about Gus vanished at the sound of Lloyd's voice. She honestly hadn't expected him to call. She couldn't deny her attraction to him, but it troubled her, and she'd done nothing to conceal her uneasiness from Lloyd. She was certain that he had been less than satisfied by the time they'd spent together over the past weekend. Surely he had plenty of women falling all over him in Hartford; why did he want to persevere with Emily?

Gus stalked to her side, and she absentmindedly scratched his rump as she considered Lloyd's statement. "What did you have in mind?" she finally asked.

"I can drive up to New Preston Friday after work," he suggested. "We can spend the weekend together."

Emily wasn't stupid—she could read between the lines. "Now who's being euphemistic?" she chided him. " 'Spend the weekend together'? I'm not going to go to bed with you." It was easier to say this with conviction over the telephone, when she didn't have to contend with his piercing eyes and his magnificent body.

He didn't respond immediately. "Emily." He exhaled. "Do you think I'd drive forty miles just to get laid? That's not why I want to see you." After a pause, he added, "I'll reserve a room at the inn if that's what you want."

Emily considered. Lloyd seemed willing to abide by her terms. Evidently he enjoyed her company enough to want to spend time with her within the limitations she'd set down. An entire weekend, boating, perhaps, swimming, tennis . . . "The tree," she abruptly reminded herself.

"What?"

"There's a dead tree in my backyard I've got to clear out this weekend."

"I can help," Lloyd volunteered. "We can work on it together."

Emily laughed. "Here you are, finally taking vacations for the first time in five years, and how do you spend them? Repairing porches and hacking down dead trees. That's not my idea of a vacation."

"It's mine," he claimed. "If I leave directly from work I should get to New Preston by about six. I'll check in and then pick you up for dinner."

"I'll plan accordingly," Emily promised.

"I'll see you then," said Lloyd.

He didn't sound particularly romantic, Emily mused as she bade him farewell and hung up the phone. That was fine with her. She had delineated the boundaries and he seemed willing to respect them. She hoped he wouldn't attempt anything physical with her. She liked Lloyd Gordon. She liked him enough to want to avoid spoiling their friendship with her own sexual inadequacies. And for whatever reason, he appeared able to accept that.

"So," she told Gus, "Lloyd's coming to visit again. You like him, too, don't you?"

Gus eyed her pathetically, then loped to the back door and rubbed his shoulder against it. He was obviously more concerned about his own love life than Emily's.

"Forget it, pal," she chided him. "Whoever she is, she's probably not good enough for you anyway."

Thinking about Lloyd's impending visit elated Emily more than she would have imagined, and she couldn't suppress her glee when she arrived at the animal hospital the following morning. "What makes you so chipper?" Tom teased her as they examined their small pharmacy, checking supplies. In his late middle years, Tom was short and balding and perpetually cheerful. He and Emily had instantly taken to each other when they'd met two years before, and by the end of an hour's interview he'd invited her to buy out his retiring partner's share of the clinic. Emily's divorce settlement had provided her with the funds to do so, and she and Tom had become fast friends since her arrival in the Litchfield Hills. Although he was old enough to be her father, he treated her as an equal, and so did his wife.

"Big date this weekend," Emily informed him. "We're running low on heartworm pills, by the way."

He made a note of it on his clipboard, then pressed Emily about her date. "Anyone I know?"

She shook her head. "He's from Hartford. He's visiting for the weekend."

"He must be pretty crazy about you if he'd travel all that distance just to see you," Tom observed.

Emily rolled her eyes in pretended annoyance. "We don't know each other well enough for him to be pretty crazy about me," she refuted. "We're just friends."

"But he's spending the weekend."

"At an inn," she stressed.

Before Tom could question her further, Sally, their assistant, appeared at the pharmacy's open door. "There's a kid in the waiting room with a limping pet turtle," she announced. "Also, Mrs. Blaine's due any minute with her weimaraner."

Relieved of having to explain her relationship with Lloyd, Emily smiled at Tom and left the pharmacy to attend to the turtle's injured leg.

The animal hospital remained busy throughout the day, and Emily didn't have the opportunity to chat with Tom again until closing time. Yet it was obvious his partner's social life was still on his mind, because as they checked their overnight patients one last time before locking up he asked, "So what do you and your big date have on tap for the weekend?"

"Chopping up that dead tree in my backyard," Emily replied. "You don't by any chance have a chain saw I can borrow, do you?"

"I haven't seen my chain saw since my son-in-law borrowed it to cut firewood last fall," Tom complained. "But you might try the hardware store in town."

"I hate to have to buy one," Emily grumbled.

"Maybe they'll rent you one for the weekend," Tom commented. "They do that with some tools."

"I'll check into it," Emily said with a nod. "Thanks for the suggestion. I've got to go there anyway to buy a new runner leash for Gus. He's outgrowing the one I've got."

She and Tom parted ways in the parking lot, and Emily drove directly into downtown Litchfield. It was a picturesque town, its rectangular green lined on one side with shops and on the other three sides with historic buildings. The town had once been a major stopping place on the route between Hartford and Albany, but in the twentieth century it had been bypassed by modern highways, and it seemed to have been frozen in a previous era. If Emily hadn't found an affordable house on Lake Waramaug, she would gladly have settled in the bucolic village.

She parked near the hardware store, pleased to find it still open. The proprietor assured her that she could rent a chain saw for the weekend, and Emily made arrangements to pick it up on Friday afternoon. Then she bought a heavy leash of woven nylon with a clip at one end. Even Gus wouldn't be able to escape from such a strong tether, she decided as she carried her purchase to her car.

She knew something was wrong as soon as she pulled into the garage and climbed out of her station wagon. She didn't hear Gus's welcoming barks. Her heart clutching slightly, she raced to her backyard. He was gone.

Cursing softly, she examined the runner leash. She'd been a day too late, she realized, as she saw the frayed end of the rope that had connected Gus's collar to the runner. He'd broken away, and undoubtedly was galloping through the woods in search of his sweetheart.

Emily cursed again. She entered her house only to drop off her purse, then darted outside and headed for the woods. She paused every few minutes to cup her hands around her mouth and yell Gus's name, but the only response she got was the frightened scampering of forest animals through the branches above her head. She forged deeper into the woods, calling and calling. But no Gus.

Sighing, she trudged back to her house in the waning light. He'd return, she tried to reassure herself. He'd find his lady friend, answer nature's call, and return home. He knew the house, and he'd been through the woods enough times to be able to get back home. There wasn't much Emily could do about it but wait for him to come home.

Yet she couldn't stop worrying. Her house seemed barren and lonely without Gus in it. She was so totally in the habit of caring for him that she automatically filled his food dish with dinner before recalling that he wasn't around to eat it. She was unable to taste her own dinner. No matter how many times she told herself that Gus was a strong, tough, independent creature, she couldn't help fretting about his disappearance.

She slept fitfully and arose before her alarm clock rang. She dashed to her front door, then to the kitchen door, hoping to find Gus outside. But he wasn't there. She left the house for a quick jog around her property, but she found no sign of her pet in the vicinity.

There wasn't a thing she could do about it, she told herself as she choked down a bowl of cereal. She had to get to work. She'd continue her search in the evening when she got home. Maybe she wouldn't have to, she thought, trying to bolster her spirits—maybe Gus would be back by then.

But he wasn't. She circled the lake in her car, hollering his name through her open window. When she finally arrived back at her house, she phoned several neighbors to ask if they'd spotted him during the day. They all said no, and helpfully promised to keep an eye out for him.

She had to force herself to eat dinner. The silence of her house grated on her, and she couldn't bear to look at the new leash she'd bought for him. She tore herself up with guilt for not having purchased the leash sooner, knowing even as she did that guilt wasn't going to bring Gus back.

He hadn't returned by Thursday, and another, longer search of the woods didn't locate him. Emily's worry marked her face, underlining her eyes with shadows and drawing the edges of her lips into a miserable frown. Even thinking about Lloyd's impending visit didn't cheer her up. She forgot all about picking up the chain saw Friday afternoon, driving directly home from work to search the woods again for her missing pet.

Tramping through the dense undergrowth, calling Gus's name and hearing only her voice's echo in reply, she nearly lost track of the time. When she remembered to glance at her watch, she was shocked to discover that it was after six. Lloyd would be arriving any minute.

She plodded back to the house, wrestling with her mood, hoping her spirits would improve before he showed up. But he was earlier than she'd expected. She had just undressed and was about to step into the shower when she heard his car's tires crunch along the unpaved driveway.

She dashed back to her bedroom and slipped on her bathrobe. Hearing Lloyd's knock on her front door, she didn't waste time checking her appearance in the mirror. She hurried through the house to the door, taking a deep breath and telling herself to cheer up. Then she swung the door open.

Lloyd stood on the porch, dressed in a pair of tan corduroy slacks and a darker brown blazer, his beige cotton shirt open at the collar. For a long moment Emily simply gaped at him, absorbing his handsome, chiseled features, his thick, luxuriously curly hair, his hypnotic blue eyes.

Then she realized that he was gaping at her too. "You aren't ready yet?" he asked, though the answer was obvious.

She opened her mouth and then closed it, trying to recover from the stunning sight of Lloyd and from the astonishingly sensual memories his presence evoked. For a moment she forgot about Gus, remembering only Lloyd's kisses, the dangerous electricity his touch elicited from within her. "No," she finally mumbled, lowering her eyes to the floor to break the spell. "No, I'm not ready yet."

He hesitantly followed her into the living room, evidently expecting Gus to spring from nowhere and tackle him. When Gus didn't appear, Lloyd shifted his eyes to Emily's unhappy face. "You look terrible," he observed.

Emily nodded. "I'll—I've got to shower, and I'll fix myself up."

Lloyd cupped his hand around her chin and lifted her face to his. "What happened?"

"Gus ran away."

He scanned the room and nodded. "When?"

"Tuesday evening. I've just been racing around the woods for the umpteenth time, looking for him."

"You've also been losing sleep," Lloyd commented, his eyes coursing over her. "You really look dreadful, Emily."

She wasn't insulted by his criticism; in fact, she was strangely heartened by it. It indicated Lloyd's sensitivity to her. "I know I look dreadful. I've been so worried, Lloyd—I don't know where Gus is. He's never disappeared like this before. I'm scared." She forced a feeble smile. "I'll try not to worry tonight. Let me just go wash up and dress."

Lloyd didn't release her. His acute eyes wandered across her face, taking in her grim expression. "You're not going to stop worrying until you find him," he guessed.

"I'll try."

He meditated for a moment, then exhaled. "Put on some jeans. We'll go out and look some more."

Lloyd's offer to assist her in her search for Gus moved Emily. He *did* like Gus; she knew it. And he liked her, too. He liked her enough to want to help her, and to forgo a dinner he knew she would be too preoccupied to enjoy. "Thank you," she whispered before hurrying back to her bedroom to dress.

Once she was clad in the clothes she'd worn at work—her faded dungarees and a plaid cotton blouse —she found Lloyd in her kitchen, fingering the new leash. "I was expecting Gus to do something like this," she explained remorsefully. "But I wasn't quick enough."

"Dogs can be such a nuisance," he muttered, pocketing the leash and opening the back door for Emily.

The sky had begun to darken, and before she stepped outside she fetched a flashlight from the cabinet beside the refrigerator. "We might need this in the woods," she noted as she led Lloyd across the yard. As soon as they entered the dim forest, she realized that his outfit was totally unsuited for hiking through the underbrush. "You're going to ruin your clothes," she said, apologizing.

"Don't worry about it," he told her, dismissing her concern. "I'll watch my step."

They prowled deeper into the woods, and Emily flicked on the flashlight, letting its beam illuminate the rugged terrain beneath their feet. Branches whipped against their arms, and stones and bulging roots thwarted them. After traveling several hundred feet, they halted and shouted Gus's name. They were greeted only by the strident cawing of a crow above their heads.

They ventured further. The dense foliage obliterated what little natural light lingered in the sky, and they cautiously slowed their pace. They called Gus's name again. Nothing.

After half an hour, Emily stopped to orient herself. "This is useless," she said with a baleful sigh. "We're not going to find him."

"You want to head back?"

"I don't want to," Emily admitted. "But I don't see the point in continuing."

Lloyd pursed his lips but remained silent. Emily didn't know whether he was angered by the turn their evening had taken or by her depression over her missing pet. Perhaps he was only saddened, as she was, by Gus's disappearance.

She turned and picked her way back in the direction of her house, Lloyd stumbling through the forest behind her. Suddenly she spotted a long, dark shadow—the back of a dog lying prone on the ground several yards away. "Gus!" she shrieked excitedly as she hurried toward the shadow. "Gussie! What happened to you?"

The shadow didn't move, for the simple reason that it was only a log. But by the time Emily had discovered that, it was too late. Her toe caught beneath the protruding root of a maple tree and she felt herself tumbling, crashing to the ground by the log.

"Emily! Are you all right?" Lloyd jogged toward her contorted body.

She pulled herself up to a sitting position and recovered her breath. The flashlight's beam struck the trunk of a tree, and she reached to grab it. The motion caused a sharp pain to shoot up her leg from her ankle. "Damn!" she groaned.

Lloyd dropped to his knees beside her. "Are you okay?"

"I turned my ankle," she muttered, sucking in her breath as she wiggled her foot free of the root. "Just a sprain."

Lloyd pulled the flashlight from her fist and turned it

on her left foot. When he rolled up the leg of her dungarees she winced. "It's swollen," he announced.

"It looks worse than it is," she assured him. "I injured it years ago. All I have to do is look at it the wrong way and it swells up."

"Emily, it's terribly puffy," he murmured. When he pressed his hand gingerly to the lump above her instep she groaned again. "Maybe I'd better take you to a doctor."

"No, it's just a sprain, really," she insisted. "I didn't hear anything crack when I fell. I twist it all the time, Lloyd. It's nothing serious."

He frowned, then handed her the flashlight. Sliding his arms beneath her knees and shoulders, he carefully lifted her off the ground. "Light the way," he ordered her.

She curled one arm around his neck and focused the flashlight's beam on the ground before them. Her head rested against his shoulder as he picked his way cautiously through the forest. His grip was strong and confident. "I'm sorry I weigh so much," she mumbled.

"You don't weigh so much," he refuted her. "You weigh just the right amount."

"The right amount to give you a hernia?" she snorted.

"The right amount to feel very nice in my arms," he answered.

Emily said nothing more. Lloyd's words sounded not seductive but comforting. She felt safe in his arms, protected. She was hardly aware of the throbbing in her ankle.

Eventually they reached her yard, and Lloyd carried her through the back door into the kitchen, where he gently deposited her on a chair. He dragged another chair over and lifted her leg onto it. Then he unlaced her sneaker and eased it and her sock off. At the sight of her misshapen ankle he grimaced.

"It looks worse than it is," she reiterated.

"What do I do with it?" Lloyd asked. "Heat or ice?"

"Ice," she said.

He nodded as he stood and removed his jacket, draping it over the back of a third chair. He rolled up the sleeves of his shirt, then scanned the room, finding a clean dish towel. Without asking Emily's permission to make himself at home in her kitchen, he crossed to her refrigerator, opened the freezer compartment, and pulled out an ice-cube tray.

Emily settled back in her chair and watched him prepare the ice pack for her. Given how self-sufficient she was, she rarely was pampered by anyone, and she enjoyed having Lloyd take care of her. He wrapped the frozen cubes inside the towel, moistened it to better conduct the ice's coldness, and then balanced it on her foot. "Would you like a pillow under your heel?" he asked.

She laughed, touched by his solicitousness. "Who needs a soaking wet pillow?"

"How about another towel, then?"

"Okay. The bathroom's down the hall."

He vanished from the kitchen, returning in less than a minute with a bath towel, which he folded into a plump cushion for her foot. "What else can I get you?" he asked. "Aspirin? A stiff drink?"

She smiled, her dark eyes sparkling with delight. "I'm fine. You make a fantastic nurse, Lloyd," she said, flattering him.

Her praise made him cringe, which surprised her. He turned back to the ice-cube tray and refilled it with water. "I guess we aren't going to go out for dinner," he remarked quietly.

His mild tension baffled Emily, but she chalked it up to his shyness. Perhaps he was unused to being complimented. Perhaps some men didn't like to be considered nurses. "I'm sure we can rustle up some food here," she told him. "You'll have to fix it, though."

"No problem." He opened her refrigerator, examined its contents, and removed a carton of eggs and a package of cheese. "Omelets?"

"Sounds great," she enthused.

Other than pointing out the cabinets that held her pans, bowls and plates, Emily didn't offer to aid him in their dinner's preparation. She simply watched him work, finding pleasure in the mere sight of him as much as in his considerateness. "You *do* make a good nurse," she praised him.

"You make a good patient," he returned.

"What's a good patient?"

He scrambled the eggs, immersed in thought for several seconds. "One who accepts help without making a big deal about it," he finally answered. He poured the eggs into a heated skillet, then moved to the cabinet where Emily stored her liquor. Evidently he remembered its location from the previous weekend, when Emily had poured him a glass of vodka. That was the drink he chose for himself again. When he held up the bottle to her, she shook her head. "I'll have a glass of milk," she said. He obediently poured one for her. "I mean it, Lloyd," she said as she accepted the glass. "If you ever want to quit the economic forecasting business, I'll hire you on full-time."

"No thanks," he grunted, returning to the stove to concentrate on the eggs. "I've had enough experience as a nurse to last me a lifetime."

His wife, Emily immediately intuited. He'd nursed his wife. She waited to speak until the omelets were cooked and Lloyd had joined her at the table. Before lifting her fork, she asked, "You took care of your wife?"

She had expected him to retort that she was being nosy, that he didn't wish to discuss his wife, but he only nodded. Encouraged, she continued with her inquiry. "Was she always depressive?"

He pondered the question for several minutes. "No," he replied hesitantly. "Not really."

"Was she under a doctor's care?"

Again she anticipated that he'd put a stop to the conversation, but he didn't. He ran his fingers through his unruly curls, then reached for his vodka and sipped. "She was under a doctor's care, yes," he stated. "Plenty of doctors, actually. Not counting the witch doctor in Utah, the herbalist in Oregon, and some quack in Florida who boasted about miracle cures brought on by snake-venom injections."

"Miracle cures?" Emily echoed, perplexed.

"There isn't a cure, of course," he said with a sigh.

"Some people—" She paused, choosing her words carefully. "Some people can be saved."

"From suicide, maybe," he allowed. "My wife had MS."

"Multiple sclerosis?"

He nodded once more, his eyes shadowed. "They haven't come up with a cure for that yet."

Emily nibbled on her omelet and organized her thoughts. Lloyd's revelation demolished all her preconceptions about his wife. The woman wasn't suicidal, then, merely sick, suffering from an incurable disease. Apparently her suicide had been caused not by mental instability but by the hopelessness of her condition. *Mercy killing,* Emily realized, struck by a memory of Lloyd's furious reaction when she'd mentioned putting the deer out of its misery the day they'd met. *Euthanasia.* Knowing what had happened to his wife explained a lot to Emily. "Oh, Lloyd," she sighed. "I'm sorry. I didn't know."

Her apology confused him. "Didn't know what?"

"Didn't know . . ." She sighed again. "About your wife. It must have been very hard for you." He

94

shrugged stoically, his eyes on his plate as he ate his meal. "How long did she have it?"

"The first symptoms appeared about three months after we were married. She had a severe case; it progressed rapidly. Within a year she couldn't walk anymore."

Emily wanted to tell him that he didn't have to talk about it, that she would respect his privacy. But he continued without any prompting from her. "She wasn't a good patient. She was too noble, Emily. She couldn't stand letting me take care of her. She was very bitter about it."

"It's one thing to sprain an ankle," Emily pointed out. "It's another thing to be confined to a wheelchair."

He seemed bitter himself. "It wouldn't have been so bad if—if she'd dealt with it differently. But she didn't. She couldn't. So we both became bitter. I took care of her and she hated me for it."

Everything came together for Emily now, all the clues Lloyd had given her about himself. No wonder he didn't like pets. He'd spent too much of his life devoting his time and attention to a woman who'd resented his efforts. As he'd said, he'd had enough nursing experience to last him a lifetime. He didn't want to take care of anyone or anything again. "You must have loved her very much," Emily whispered.

His eyes shot up, capturing hers with their hard brilliance. Then they softened and he let out a slow breath. He reached for his glass and drank. "Love didn't have much to do with it," he said.

"But to care for her that way—"

"She was my wife," he explained tersely, then relented. "She probably would have been happier if I'd left her."

"No, of course not!" Emily objected groundlessly.

He raised his eyes to her again, but they were steady, devoid of emotion. "She grew to despise me, Emily.

95

She despised me because I was a constant reminder of how helpless she was. I kept my job with the government because of the insurance benefits and the security, and she knew I loathed the work, and there was just so much resentment. . . ." He drank again. "Love is an entirely different thing from what we had. Love has to do with sharing experiences, repairing porches, and playing tennis together. Boating. Sex. Arguing."

"You didn't—argue?" Emily asked tactfully.

He noticed the catch in her voice and smiled wryly. "No, we didn't argue. We didn't have sex either."

"She couldn't?"

"She wouldn't. She hated her body. She urged me to satisfy myself by having an affair."

Curiosity overcame tact. "Did you?" Emily blurted out.

He shook his head. "What an opportunity," he muttered sardonically. "I had the classic line: 'My wife's in a wheelchair. I can't leave her, but I can't love her.' No, I didn't have an affair. I'm not that kind of man."

Of course he wasn't; Emily knew that instinctively. Lloyd was too decent, too restrained. "You . . . you said you went boating with her."

He nodded. "Yes, I put her in a boat and rowed her around the lake. She hated it. After all of ten minutes she asked me to take her back to the cabin."

"Why did you come here?" Emily inquired softly. "I mean, last week. Why did you come back to the lake?"

He fingered his glass, his eyes distant as he reflected. "I don't know," he murmured. "I guess . . . I was tired of eating myself up. I wanted to get it out of my system. Five years was long enough." He drained his glass, his eyes still glazed with memory. "I brought her here because I thought it would save her. She was deteriorating badly, having vision problems, starting to lose the use of her arms. I thought if we went away for a while, if we could just unwind and forget everything for a couple of weeks . . . But it didn't happen. After a week she wanted to go home. And I knew it was the end."

"You knew she was going to die?"

"I knew . . . I knew she was ready to die," he declared, his voice barely above a whisper. He stared at Emily's hands, folded beside her plate, unable to look directly at her. "She took painkillers, Emily. She asked me to leave them by her night table. The day nurse always kept them in the bathroom, but one evening when I got home from work she asked me to bring them to her. She could still use her hands, she said. One thing she could do for herself was take her medication." A shaky breath filtered from his lungs. "She asked me to buy her some ice cream. And she asked me to leave her pills for her in case she needed them while I was out. I might be gone a while, she told me. She wanted a particular brand of ice cream, a particular flavor that was hard to find." He bent his elbows and rested his face in his hands. "Oh, Emily, Emily," he breathed. "I left her the pills and I went. I drove all over Hartford looking for her damned ice cream. I knew what she was going to do and I left. I let her do it."

Emily was afraid he would cry. She almost hoped he would. But he didn't. He stared bleakly past her, his fingers spread across his cheeks, his eyes dry and his face drained of color. "You did the right thing," she said to console him.

Slowly his gaze moved to her, searching her face. "When you asked me last week—in the garage—when you asked me if I'd killed her, I . . . I almost cried out that I had. Saying that, Emily, accusing me of that—you nearly made me lose my mind."

"I know." She recalled the frightening look on his face that afternoon, the look that had so shaken her she'd had to run away. "Lloyd, if you never forgave me for saying that, I wouldn't blame you."

"I've already forgiven you," he said quietly.

She mulled over what Lloyd had told her. Her heart brimmed with sympathy for what he'd been through, and her mind twisted in confusion as to why he'd suddenly decided to share his story with her. "Why have you told me all this?" she asked.

He studied her thoughtfully. "Because you're brave," he answered. "Because you're strong. Because you're the first person I've ever met who was brave enough and strong enough to force it out of me."

"Are you sorry you've told me?"

"No," he promised. "No, I'm not."

A heady warmth rippled through her. She had succeeded with Lloyd. She'd broken through the ice, saved him from the anguished past that had frozen him. She'd cured him. He'd trusted her, opened up to her, let her free him. And she loved him for it.

She loved him. The startling recognition rocked her soul. Never before had a man trusted her so much. Never before had a man bared himself to her as Lloyd had. The silly confessions of the people she'd known when she was married to Ed—and Ed's confessions, as well—were so trivial, so inane and meaningless. Ed had deliberately introduced Emily to his first mistress, and then his second, because he was secretly proud of his infidelities. He hadn't done it to be honest, but rather to flaunt his dishonesty.

But not Lloyd. Lloyd had opened up to her because he needed to, because he needed her. She was overwhelmed by the understanding of what existed between them.

She wanted to hold him. She wanted to hold him and kiss him and tell him that she loved him for trusting her, for giving her his pain to cure. "Why don't we—" Her voice trembled, and she swallowed to steady it. "Why don't we clean up and then relax in the living room?"

Lloyd refused to let her help him wash the dishes. Once the kitchen was clean, he assisted her onto her right foot and helped her hobble into the living room, where they sat side by side on the couch. Emily propped her sprained ankle on the coffee table and Lloyd curled his arm around her. She nestled her head into his shoulder. "Thank you," she murmured.

"For what?"

"For trusting me."

He turned to her, studying her in the amber light from the lamp beside the sofa. His eyes grew soft, a sweet, liquid blue, as he leaned toward her, moving his lips over her forehead. She tilted back her head and their mouths met.

The blaze of Lloyd's passion swept through Emily, familiar though no less awesome in its power than before. Yet it seemed stronger to her tonight. Now she knew she loved him, and that knowledge fed the flame, directing it through her until her soul caught fire.

She didn't think about her past failures. She didn't think about her inability to respond to men. She loved Lloyd, and she was convinced that her love alone would cure her, as his trust in her had cured him.

She slid her fingers deep into the tangled curls that covered his head, and he eased her onto her back, adjusting himself above her. "Emily," he sighed, his mustache brushing her chin as he kissed it. "We don't have to do this."

"Yes, we do," she murmured. Her voice seemed to have vanished, all her energy concentrated deep inside her, arousing her nerves until they bristled with the heat of her desire.

"Are you sure?"

"I'm sure."

Her hands confirmed her words, running down his back to his waist, past his belt to his hips. She pressed him to herself and a low, incoherent sound wrenched loose from his throat. "I want you," he groaned.

"I want you too."

His hands shook slightly as he fumbled with the buttons of her blouse. They fell open, and his lips touched the hollow at the base of her throat. Emily's stomach clenched, and for the first time in her life she understood that her body wanted a man as much as her mind did. Not just a man—one man. Lloyd. Lloyd Gordon.

He fingered the front clasp of her bra and unclipped it, pushing the fabric away, sliding both her blouse and her bra down her arms and out from under her. Leaning back on his haunches, he surveyed her full white breasts before setting his hands free to explore the creamy expanse. "Promise me you'll never go on a diet," he demanded.

"You *do* like full-figured women, don't you?" she teased.

"One woman's figure in particular."

"I guess that's only to be expected from a man who came of age reading *Playboy*," she mocked him.

He smiled briefly, then lowered his mouth to her breast. Her throat closed about her laughter as shock waves of sensation rippled through her at his provocative kisses. His tongue circled her nipple, drawing it out until it was a hard bud, ripe for the tender assault of his lips.

Her hands clutched his head, holding him snugly to her. Her fingers twined through the soft black curls and she closed her eyes, savoring the sheer force of her body's intense reaction to him. She felt more at this moment than she'd ever felt before, readier, surer of herself. Her soul seemed to blossom open, a delicate natural flowering. She wouldn't fail this time. She knew it. Lloyd would open her as she'd opened him.

Her hands slid down to his shirt, tugging it from the waistband of his trousers. He leaned back to unbutton it, then shrugged it off and tossed it to the floor. Her fingers traced the width of his shoulders, then traveled forward to his chest, dancing through the silky black hair. His small, dark nipples tautened before she had even touched them. Just the nearness of her fingers aroused them as her hands floated down to his rock-hard abdomen.

"Emily." His voice was thick and hoarse with long-ing. He reached for the fly of her jeans and opened it, then peeled both her slacks and her panties over her hips. He rose above her to ease the jeans down her legs, gingerly passing the denim over her inflamed ankle. "Does it hurt?" he asked.

"No," she told him. She was aware of no pain, only a deep, throbbing ache, a fierce hunger for Lloyd.

"I could tape it or something."

"No." She couldn't stand the thought of his leaving her for even the few minutes it would take to attend to her ankle.

He lifted his eyes to her and read her yearning. He bowed his head and gently kissed the swelling around her anklebone, then stood to remove the remainder of his clothing.

She devoured his beautiful body with her eyes. The breadth of his chest, the lean tapering of his hips, the glory of his arousal only increased her excitement. He lowered himself back onto her, letting one hand stroke the length of her thighs before rising to touch her feminine heart.

She gasped. A part of her argued that this couldn't be real, that what she was feeling wasn't possible. But another part of her insisted that it *was* real, that anything in the entire world was possible, that Lloyd had turned possibility into truth. "Love me," she breathed, dazed by her building passion. "Now. Please . . ."

He obliged, withdrawing his hand and fusing his body to hers. And it continued, her body's eagerness; it continued, the fire rising through her, the heat com-pounding itself as Lloyd moved inside her. She closed her eyes, surrendering to his dazzling thrusts, to her own heavenly awakening.

Then she reached a plateau, hovering, suspended, waiting. And suddenly her body began to cool, the sublime sensation ebbing before it had a chance to reach its peak. *No*, she wailed silently, trying to cling to the elusive feeling, knowing even as she tried that her efforts were useless. Once again the promise would not be fulfilled. Once again her body would fail her.

She opened her eyes to find Lloyd's face looming above hers. His eyelids were lowered, his brow beaded with dampness, the tendons in his neck visible as he labored to contain himself. She wanted to tell him that he shouldn't bother, that he should give himself over to his own pleasure because no willpower on his part would change what had happened to her. But she liked the feel of him inside her; she liked the precious closeness she felt with him this way. She wanted that to remain.

She shut her eyes again, detecting his subtly changing pace. He surged deeper within her, more powerfully, and when her hands cupped his hips she felt his muscles tensing. He stopped breathing for an instant, then succumbed to his own ecstatic release, filling her with himself. His breath escaped in a low, ragged moan.

He settled heavily on her, and she let her fingers waltz up to his waist, taking comfort in his weight, in his solid shape. His tongue drew a line along her shoulder, and then he kissed the moisture away.

"I'm sorry," he whispered.

"No. Don't be."

He propped himself up on his elbows, peering down at her face. His fingers combed hesitantly through her hair, brushing it from her cheeks. "Does your ankle hurt?"

"No."

"You're worried about Gus?"

She realized with a small pang that she'd forgotten all about Gus. But she knew Lloyd was searching for a justification for what had happened, any justification but the obvious one—that she simply wasn't able to respond to him at the ultimate moment.

She dared to meet his eyes, and their troubled silver-blue cut through her. She twisted her head to stare at the intricate tweed pattern of her sofa's bolster. "Don't be sorry, Lloyd," she muttered. "It was lovely. Really. I enjoyed it."

He didn't move for a long time. She knew he was staring at her, gauging her, trying to figure out what had gone wrong. She silently thanked him for not questioning her. He was more discreet than she was; he wouldn't probe about her discomfort. He only watched her, his eyes trying to penetrate the icy shell Emily felt closing around herself.

6

After a long while he stood. He tucked his arms beneath her and scooped her off the couch. Her mouth was dry, her tongue numbed by her chagrin. She didn't ask him what he was doing, but only snuggled close to him, seeking strength from his embrace.

He carried her directly to her bedroom. She realized that he must have discovered its location when he went to the bathroom to fetch a towel for her ankle earlier that evening. The open curtains allowed the shimmering silver radiance of the night's half moon to filter into the room, and Lloyd didn't bother to turn on the light.

He placed her gently on the bed, then stretched out beside her, his arms folded around her shoulders. She prayed he wouldn't say anything and he answered her prayers, merely leaning down to kiss her.

His lips felt comforting on hers. One of his hands rose to journey through her hair and the other glided the length of her body, reaching her knee and then returning to her throat, down again and then up in a soothing rhythm that consoled her. Gradually her frustration began to fade.

Lloyd let his hand settle between her legs and touch her. Her eyes hardened and she shrank back from him. "Don't," she protested nervously, trying to shift her hips away from his hand. She couldn't bear to be disappointed again.

He grazed her chin with his mouth. "Trust me," he whispered. "Close your eyes and relax." Although dubious, she complied, letting her head sink back against the down pillow. His fingers stroked her sensitive flesh, as light as a breath of air.

His lips slid down her throat to her breast, then closed about her nipple. He sucked it tenderly, and she felt as if a slack cord connecting her breast to her womb had begun to coil tight. A fleeting thought of motherhood passed hazily through her mind, then evanesced.

The moist friction of his lips against her nipple increased almost imperceptibly. She concentrated on the sensation, and the cord pulled tighter, thickening, multiplying itself. She wasn't aware that her legs had moved until she felt a dull ache in her sprained left ankle. She willed her feet to remain motionless, and her thighs moved instead.

She felt no fire, no blaze roaring through her flesh. Instead she felt only a tension inside her, a tugging, a contracting. Lloyd's motions became more insistent, and her consciousness of his mouth blended with that of his continuous stroking. The pain in her ankle disappeared, her feet arching and her toes curling inward. She tried to obey Lloyd and relax, but she couldn't. Her body was seized by an anxious tautness that drove her up, up, and out of herself, away.

Her hips writhed, seeking a release from the sensation that gripped her. She heard an alien sound—her own voice, choked and moaning. It was no stranger to her than the agonizing pressure inside her, driving her further, forcing her toward a crest. She reached it in a devastating surge and rode it, the cord suddenly snapping and hurling energy in rapturous pulses through her flesh.

She was still moaning when Lloyd lifted his mouth from her breast and opened it against hers. What she'd endured exhausted her, but not him. He caressed her, still stroking, and she felt the pressure return, deeper and stronger, swiftly conquering her body and driving her over another crest. Her astonished cry filled Lloyd's mouth.

An eternity seemed to pass before her flesh stopped throbbing, before her body settled against the mattress with a sweet shudder. She turned to Lloyd and cuddled up to him, seeking the protection of his warmth, weeping quietly into his chest. He held her, his hands cupping her trembling shoulders, his lips calming her as they wandered through her hair.

"I used to think—" She sighed, still shaking slightly. "I used to think there was something wrong with me."

"There's nothing wrong with you," he murmured. "Not a single thing."

She buried her lips in the soft swirls of hair that covered his chest. She wondered whether Lloyd understood what he had done for her. He had to, she realized. He had to know. There was no need to tell him in words.

Her mind toyed with the image of an ice cube submerged in hot water. She pictured the way such an ice cube shatters from the inside, splintering as it expands against itself. That was how she felt now, externally unchanged but completely altered from within, her soul sparkling with countless facets of light, like a jewel. Lloyd was the warmth into which she'd been submerged. He had asked her to trust him, and then he had reached beyond her surface of ice to transform her.

And she had done as much for him. She'd won his trust, warmed him, broken through.

She thought about his wife, about the bitterness of his past. Emily could hardly guess how she would have reacted to a disease as debilitating as his wife's. Yet she couldn't help thinking that if she was ever forced to face such an ordeal, she would want Lloyd beside her to share it with her. She would never resent him. She would gladly lean on him, trust him, turn to him, rely on his strength when hers faltered.

He was so kind, so generous. So selfless. Certainly he hadn't become that way overnight. He must always have been a decent, caring man. His wife's inability to accept his love had forced him to bury it so deeply that only a woman as brave—or as foolhardy—as Emily could smash down the emotional wall of reserve he had constructed around himself to recover his soul.

Emily's relationship with Ed hadn't endured the vicissitudes of Lloyd's relationship with his wife, but like Lloyd's, it had defeated her. It had convinced her that she was somehow to blame for her inability to cope with her spouse's behavior. She had believed that it was her failure to adjust to Ed that had destroyed their relationship. She had loved Ed, but he hadn't been able to accept the love she offered. And the marriage had died.

But now she had found a man who accepted who she was and what she was, who thought her body was beautiful, who appreciated her lack of pretense. She'd found a man who had willingly tapped into her soul to mine its treasures. She didn't have to tell Lloyd this. She was certain that he knew it.

He shifted on the mattress and sat up. Emily possessively grasped his arm and pleaded, "No! Don't go."

He turned to her and smiled. "I'm only pulling up the

blanket," he explained, reaching for the lightweight comforter folded at the foot of the bed. He draped it over their bodies, then settled himself beside her again. They faced each other, sharing the pillow, their eyes communicating their shimmering bliss. "You don't want me to leave?" he asked hesitantly.

"No."

"I've got a room at the inn, you know," he reminded her.

"You've got a room here," she insisted.

He couldn't resist teasing her. "My clothing is there."

"We'll pick it up tomorrow."

"Okay. Because assuming I didn't ruin my slacks tonight, I don't want to chop wood in them."

"The tree," she remembered. "I have to pick up a chain saw in Litchfield tomorrow, too. We'll get your clothes and then get the saw."

"If I check out of the inn we won't be able to use their tennis court," Lloyd pointed out.

"I can't play tennis on a sprained ankle," Emily pointed out, then smiled bashfully. "We'll find something else to do," she assured him.

Lloyd's lips spread in a smile to match hers. "I'm sure we will," he whispered before kissing her brow.

He rolled onto his back, drawing her close to him. She rested her head against his shoulder, oddly pleased that he didn't choose to make love to her again. Right now she wanted to reflect on what she'd experienced, to absorb her new discovery about herself. She was normal. She was as successful as Lloyd's lover as she was in all the other aspects of her life. She no longer had to view herself as an incomplete woman. Ed's cruel accusations about her were baseless. With a man like Lloyd she could accomplish anything. Everything in the world was indeed possible.

She drifted into a contented slumber, her mind bathed by joyous dreams as her skin was bathed by the heat of Lloyd's body next to her. She could have slept in his arms forever, but shortly after dawn an eerie whining noise dragged her awake.

Lloyd reacted to her stirring by opening his eyes. She waited and heard the whining again. "Gus!" she exclaimed.

Before Lloyd could speak Emily was out of the bed. She had forgotten about her sprained ankle, and when she put her weight on it a sharp twinge shot up her leg. Ignoring the pain, she limped to her closet and groped through it for her bathrobe. Slipping it on, she hurried from the room.

The front porch was empty, and she raced to the kitchen. She swung the back door wide open, and Gus crawled over the threshold and collapsed.

"Oh my God," she gasped. "Oh Gus, what happened to you?"

He was only semiconscious, his eyes unfocused and his ribs pumping erratically. One of his rear legs was covered with blood. He barely had the strength to extend his tongue and lick her palm. Then he groaned and closed his eyes.

"Gus." A dry sob scraped through her throat. She dropped to her knees on the linoleum floor and cradled his head in her lap. "Oh Gus, Gussie, my sweet baby, what happened? What happened to you?" But she knew too well, merely by looking at his crushed paw, what had happened to him. She had seen injuries like this before, and her horror at his condition was quickly overtaken by anger.

She heard footsteps behind her and turned to find Lloyd entering the kitchen. He had wrapped the blanket around his naked body, apparently not knowing what to expect. He squatted down beside Emily, peered at Gus's quivering body, at his mangled leg, and then at Emily. "Is he all right?"

"No, he's not all right," she snapped, then touched

Lloyd's hand remorsefully. "I'm sorry, Lloyd—I'm upset."

"What happened to his leg? It looks awful."

"He must have gotten it caught in a steel-jaw trap. They're all over the woods. He must have gotten caught in one."

"I thought those things were outlawed."

"In some states," she informed him with a grim nod. "But that doesn't keep hunters from using them. The woods around here are filled with animals that have valuable fur. It's hard to catch the creeps when they're setting their traps."

Lloyd opened his mouth, then checked the impulse to speak, turning back to Gus and running his hand along the dog's heaving ribs. Once again he flexed his mouth, then murmured cautiously, "I've always heard that when animals are trapped in those things they bite their legs off to escape."

"They do sometimes," Emily confirmed softly. "Wild animals do. Domesticated animals don't. They haven't got the same survival instinct that wild animals possess." She sank onto the floor and tried to smother another sob. "I can't believe it, Lloyd—my baby, my Gussie—I can't believe this happened to him! If only I'd bought that damned leash sooner—"

Lloyd touched a finger to her lips to silence her. Then he unwrapped the blanket from his body and covered Gus with it. "How do you suppose he got out of the trap?"

"The trapper probably freed him," she muttered, tucking the blanket around Gus. "He probably found Gus in his trap and released him."

"Then why didn't he bring Gus home?" Lloyd asked ingenuously. "You've got your address on his license tag, haven't you?"

"If the hunter brought him here I'd have had him arrested before he knew what hit him," she commented. "The people who use those traps may be creeps, but they aren't stupid." She crawled to Gus's leg to examine it more closely. Her touch made Gus twitch and whimper. "It's bad, Lloyd," she murmured, her voice tremulous. "His bones are crushed." Her knowledge and experience as a veterinarian seemed to evaporate at the sight of her wounded pet, and she grimaced and turned away.

Lloyd squeezed her shoulder and stood. He left the room and returned a few minutes later carrying some towels. "You want to wrap his leg up?"

"Oh," she mumbled dully. "I ought to splint it first." She forced herself to function, shaking off her horror by clicking into a professional mind-set. "There are some magazines on the coffee table in the living room," she told Lloyd. "Would you bring them to me?"

Lloyd dutifully left to fetch the magazines, and Emily limped to the drawer where she stored string. When Lloyd presented the magazines to her, she rolled them into stiff tubes and set them on either side of Gus's leg, using the string to tie them onto the injured limb. Then she swaddled the leg in the towels Lloyd had brought her, heedless of the smears of blood that stained her floor.

"We should get him to your animal clinic," Lloyd recommended.

"Yes, of course." She nodded faintly. "I can't do anything for him here."

Lloyd helped her to her feet and examined her face. "You have a partner, right?"

"Tom Henderson. Why?"

"Maybe you ought to call him."

"It's Saturday morning. Seven o'clock," she noted, her eyes flitting to the wall clock above her sink.

"Doctors don't treat their own families," Lloyd remarked gently. "I think you ought to call him."

She nodded again, silently thanking Lloyd for being

logical when she was so dazed. She moved to the phone and dialed Tom's number. His wife answered. "Irene? It's Emily," Emily identified herself to the sleepy woman. "I woke you up. I'm sorry." Her voice cracked, and she swallowed down the lump of tears that lodged in her throat. "Is Tom there?"

"What's wrong?" Irene asked. "Are you all right, Emily? You sound terrible."

"Let me talk to Tom," Emily begged, her mind concentrated fully on Gus. She couldn't possibly pause to make small talk with Irene.

Irene didn't question her further. Several seconds elapsed, and then Emily heard Tom's sleep-fogged voice: "Emily?"

"Tom, I hate to bother you, but Gus . . ." She choked back another sob. "He's been hurt, Tom, and I don't know if I can handle it."

"I'll be at the hospital in fifteen minutes," Tom instantly offered. He knew how much Emily adored her dog, and he didn't waste time in questioning her about what sort of emergency would have prompted her to call him so early on a Saturday morning. "Meet me there." The line went dead.

Emily hung up the phone and turned to find Lloyd in the doorway, his trousers already on. He shrugged his arms through the sleeves of his shirt and buttoned it as he approached her. "Go get dressed," he ordered. "I'll stay with Gus." She nodded again, gratitude pouring from her damp eyes though she was too stupefied to give voice to it. Lloyd watched her limp to the doorway and called out after her, "Bind your ankle." She nodded again and left the room.

In a fog, she dressed in her old jeans and a T-shirt. Then she hobbled to the bathroom and pulled an Ace bandage from the medicine cabinet. Once she'd taped her ankle securely, she returned to her bedroom to don socks and sneakers. She almost forgot to brush her hair, but a glimpse of herself in the mirror displayed the tangled reddish mop to her, and she returned to the bureau to run her brush through her tresses a few times.

Back in the kitchen, she found Lloyd sitting beside Gus, rubbing the dog's snout thoughtfully. He didn't seem quite comfortable, but Emily appreciated the apparently genuine affection he was showing for her ailing pet. All his assertions about disliking dogs, about their being a nuisance, were disproved by his tender vigil over Gus.

"Let's go," she announced. "Tom said he'd meet us at the hospital."

Lloyd stood and lifted Gus from the floor. Gus groaned plaintively. "It's okay, Gussie, it's okay," Emily cooed, massaging Gus's neck as Lloyd carried him through the house to the front door. "We'll take my car," Emily decided when Lloyd started toward his BMW.

He didn't argue. She opened the rear door of her station wagon and Lloyd eased the dog inside. "Where are your keys?" he asked Emily as she closed the door and started around the car. "I'll drive."

"No, Lloyd, I'm all right," she protested.

Whether or not he believed her, he insisted on driving. "You can sit in the backseat and comfort him," he told her, pulling the keys from her hand.

Emily did as she was told, climbing into the backseat and resting on her knees so she could reach Gus's head. She continued to massage his feverish nose and throat as Lloyd backed the car down the driveway past his BMW and onto the road. He had to remind Emily to give him directions.

He found the hospital without much difficulty. Tom's car was already in the lot when they parked near the front door. Lloyd carried Gus inside the building. They found Tom, unshaven and rumpled, pacing in the loungelike waiting room. He gave Lloyd a brief, curious perusal before confronting Emily. One look at her dismal expression inspired him to gather her to himself in a compassionate hug. "You okay, Emily?"

"Yeah, sure," she replied without conviction.

"Why are you limping?"

"Forget about me. It's Gus I'm worried about."

"Right." Tom released her, then turned to Lloyd again. "You want to bring him in back?"

Lloyd followed Tom into one of the examining rooms beyond the waiting room, and Emily belatedly remembered to introduce the men. "Tom, this is Lloyd Gordon. Lloyd, Tom Henderson, my partner."

"So you're the fellow visiting for the weekend?" Tom asked Lloyd. Emily recognized that he was attempting to make light conversation to distract her from her concern about Gus, but she bristled at his prying nonetheless.

"That's right," Lloyd agreeably responded. "I wanted you to take care of this animal, because Emily is in no condition."

"I'm in perfectly fine condition," she defended herself. "I'm as good a vet as Tom is."

Tom smiled indulgently. "Emily, sweetheart, shut up," he gently commanded her. As soon as Lloyd had lowered Gus to the examining table, Tom efficiently peeled away the blanket and then the towels covering his foot. He cursed. "Jaw trap? Jesus. I'd love to see some of those hunters get caught in their own traps and see how much they like it." Before touching Gus, he crossed to a counter and gathered up a syringe and a vial of medication.

"What are you giving him?" Emily demanded.

"Painkiller, Emily," Tom replied, surprised by Emily's question. He eyed her acutely, then turned to Lloyd. "Why don't you two go out and get some breakfast? I'll look after Gus."

"I'm not going anywhere," Emily announced, embarrassed at having asked Tom such an elementary question. She should have known that an animal in as much pain as Gus required tranquilizing before his examination. Her stupid question had only illustrated how agitated she was, how unable to assist Tom in treating her pet.

Lloyd overrode her, planting his hand on her arm and steering her from the room. "A nice long breakfast," he declared, his firm tone leaving no room for argument. "We'll check back with you in a while," he called over his shoulder.

"Thanks," Tom said as Lloyd guided Emily from the room. "Get her drunk or something."

"You're not going to get me drunk," Emily muttered through gritted teeth as Lloyd led her out of the building.

"Of course not," Lloyd assured her. "I'm just going to keep you occupied for a couple of hours."

"A couple of hours?"

He nudged her into the passenger seat of the station wagon and took the wheel himself. "Where can we get some breakfast?"

"I'm not hungry."

He shot her a look that hinted at mild impatience. "Left turn or right?" he persisted.

"Right," she grunted, sinking against the upholstery. She shut her eyes and pictured her tortured dog sprawled out on the examining table, his contorted leg oozing blood onto the protective paper beneath him. Another sob crowded her throat, and she turned her face from Lloyd so he wouldn't see how despondent she was.

They drove into downtown Litchfield, and Emily listlessly pointed out a coffee shop to Lloyd. He had no trouble parking near the café, since it was the only place open at that hour along the green. They entered the charmingly decorated restaurant, and Emily cringed.

She was in no mood to be cheered up by the checkered curtains, the matching tablecloths, the quaint wrought-iron chairs and circular tables designed to evoke the picture of a turn-of-the-century ice-cream parlor.

A grinning waitress, oblivious to Emily's sullen mood, seated them and handed them two menus. Emily stared blindly at the menu, grimacing at the gay "Good morning!" scrawled across the top of the card. None of the offerings looked at all appetizing to her. Simply reading the listings made her mildly nauseous. She set down the menu.

"What do you want?" Lloyd asked.

"A cup of coffee."

He nodded and beckoned to the waitress. "We'll have . . ." He scanned the menu. "A plate of scrambled eggs, with a side order of bacon. An order of French toast. Orange juice." He glanced at Emily, then added, "And two coffees." The waitress jotted down the order, scooped up their menus, and departed.

"I hope you don't intend to make me eat any of that," Emily grumpily scolded Lloyd.

"The eggs are for you," he stated definitely. Before she could argue, he continued, "Starving yourself isn't going to help Gus. You know how to eat a hearty breakfast. I've seen you do it before."

"I'm really not hungry," she maintained.

Lloyd remained adamant. "You still have to eat." He reached across the table and took her hand, his gentle clasp contradicting his stern expression. "If you're as good a vet as Tom is, then he's as good a vet as you are. He'll do what he can for Gus."

"Lloyd, you don't understand," she protested. "I've seen this sort of thing before. The reason people want the jaw traps banned is because they injure so many pets. I've seen it too often. I know what happens to animals who get caught in the traps."

116

"What happens?"

"Usually we amputate," she said brokenly. "Sometimes . . . sometimes we have no choice but to put the animals out of—" She bit her lip, unable to finish the sentence.

"Their misery," Lloyd concluded. His tone was dry and noncommittal. "You kill them, Emily, right? It's kinder than letting them suffer."

She couldn't decipher his attitude. Was he mocking her? Ridiculing her for her pious claims the day his car had struck the deer? Or was he serious, reminding her that Tom would do what was best for Gus? The solid warmth of his hand around hers was belied by the cryptic silver glimmer in his eyes. She opened her mouth to question him but was interrupted by the arrival of the waitress with their juice and coffee.

Lloyd released her hand so she could reach for her juice. He ignored his, watching her as she lifted the glass. She forced down a mouthful, then countered his steely gaze with her own. "What do you want me to say, Lloyd? I love my dog! I don't want him to die!"

"Of course you don't," Lloyd concurred readily.

"Then why are you staring at me that way?"

He ran his hand impatiently through his mussed curls, then drank his juice in one long swallow. Lowering the empty glass to the table, he fixed his gaze on Emily. "I only want you to be prepared for what might happen. I know you love Gus, but if he dies, he dies. You can hope for the best, but you should be prepared for the worst."

Emily sank into a dejected silence. The waitress delivered their food. As soon as she was gone, Emily determinedly lifted her fork and attacked her eggs. They were tasteless to her, and they seemed to stick in her throat. She tossed down her fork and groaned. "I don't want this," she said with a sigh.

"You've got to eat something," Lloyd gently urged her. "You'll need your strength if we're going to chop apart that tree in your yard."

"The hell with the tree!"

His eyes locked with hers once more. "Listen to me, Emily. There's nothing you can do for Gus right now. Nothing. So we're going to get the saw and chop up the tree. And then maybe we'll take the canoe out. Or we'll sit on the porch and admire the lake. Or we'll play cards. Or watch TV."

"Lloyd, I'm not going to saw a tree when my dog—"

"Emily." He sounded exasperated and unyielding. "Emily, we're going to saw the tree. Don't fight me about this. You know I'm right." His voice softened slightly, and his eyes, his entire manner grew more subdued. "Please don't fight me."

Her gaze met his and she remembered everything he had ever told her about himself, about his marriage, about his wife's inability to accept his help and his love. She recognized that Lloyd was taking charge now out of love for her, and she relented with a meek sigh. "Okay," she murmured. "We'll chop the tree."

Lloyd didn't smile, but she read his satisfaction in his expressive eyes. He turned his attention to his French toast, and Emily forced herself to eat the rest of her eggs.

By the time they were finished with their breakfast, the hardware store up the block had opened, and Emily and Lloyd walked there to get her rented chain saw. Then they climbed back into her car and drove south. Nearing the animal hospital, Emily spotted a second car in the lot, parked next to Tom's. "Are you open on the weekends?" Lloyd asked as, at Emily's insistence, he steered into the lot.

"Only emergencies. That's Sally's car."

"Is she another vet?"

"She's our assistant. Tom must have called and asked

her to come in. He needs help." Before Lloyd could switch off the engine, Emily was out of the car and tearing toward the building in a lopsided jog, trying to favor her sprained ankle.

She raced through the waiting room to the door leading into the back rooms of the hospital. Evidently Sally and Tom had heard her entering the building because Sally intercepted Emily just inside the doorway. "Tom's working on him," the grandmotherly woman informed Emily. "Why don't you go on home? He'll call you when he's done."

Emily ignored Sally's advice. "How is Gus?" she asked breathlessly. "How is my dog? How is he doing?"

"He's hanging in there."

"The leg? Can Tom save it?"

"He thinks so. Now run along home." Sally's eyes drifted past Emily to study Lloyd, who loomed behind her. "You've obviously got better things to do than stay around here climbing the walls and driving Tom crazy."

"He must need assistance," Emily observed. "Why did he call you in?"

"Because he likes the sound of my voice. Run along now, Emily. Gus is going to be fine."

Emily slumped, then nodded. "Promise you'll call as soon as Tom's done?"

"The very minute," Sally swore, patting Emily's arm affectionately. "Now get out of here."

Emily turned, trying to ignore the look Sally and Lloyd exchanged. She trudged out of the building, Lloyd behind her, and climbed into the car, taking the wheel. "I'm driving," she announced morosely.

"Emily—"

"It's my car and I'm driving," she declared. For heaven's sake, she didn't need to be babied. She knew what communication Sally and Lloyd had tacitly exchanged in the animal hospital: Sally had asked Lloyd to take care of Emily, and Lloyd had promised to do just that. As if she couldn't take care of herself, as if she was too disturbed even to drive her car. She slammed the driver's-side door shut and shouted through the open window: "Get in."

Lloyd glared at her but didn't argue with her. He stalked around the front of the car and slid onto the seat beside her. He stewed without speaking as she coasted out of the parking lot.

"Why are you angry with me?" she accused him. "What did I do to you?"

"Nothing," he muttered, his gaze shifting to the road before them. He fell silent for a moment, then remarked, "I take back what I said last night about your being a good patient."

"I'm not a patient at all!" Emily retorted. "Why are you treating me like one?"

His face tensed but he said nothing. Emily felt coldness emanating toward her from his side of the car.

"Damn it, Lloyd, what do you want from me?"

"Nothing," he sighed roughly.

Her vision began to blur as tears filled her eyes. She was crying not over Gus but over Lloyd, over his retreat from her, his pulling back and closing up again. She tried to bat the tears away but they spilled over her lids, and she veered onto the shoulder of the road and stopped the car. She buried her face in her hands and wept.

Lloyd drew her across the seat and closed his arms around her. "Talk to me," he whispered.

His embrace felt so consoling, melting her, encouraging her to cry freely. He hadn't withdrawn from her after all. He was holding her, wasn't he? "It's all my fault," she sobbed.

"What's all your fault?"

"I should have bought the leash sooner. I had plenty of warning that something like this would happen. I should have bought the stronger leash before it was too late."

Lloyd's hands moved over her back, absorbing her wrenching sobs. Her shoulders heaved spasmodically, and dampness spread across his shirt from her tears.

"Tell me it's not my fault," she implored him weakly. "Tell me Gus is going to be all right."

"I'm not going to lie to you, Emily," he murmured, his lips close to her forehead, his breath cooling her skin. "Maybe it was your fault. Maybe Gus won't be all right. I don't know." He kissed the crease between her eyebrows, smoothing it with his lips. "I'll tell you something else. If you want to cry, I'm here. If you want to be held, I'll hold you. But if you want to hate me for helping, Emily . . . I'll go away. Do you understand?"

Yes. She understood. Lloyd was the sort of man who needed to be needed, and now, more than ever, Emily needed him. She could never resent him for doing his best to help her. She could never hate him for his kindness.

She nodded, her face rubbing against his shirt. "Don't go away," she requested brokenly.

"I won't," he vowed. "I won't."

7

~oececececece~

They drove to the inn. Emily accompanied Lloyd inside, taking a seat on one of the parlor's chintz sofas while he conferred with the desk clerk. After a few minutes he crossed the room to Emily. "Did you check out?" she asked.

"No," he replied. "Even if I check out, I've got to pay for the room. Cancellations have to be made forty-eight hours in advance if you want your money back. So I may as well use the room tonight."

Emily dropped her gaze. She had been sure he'd want to spend the night with her; his decision to keep his hotel room crushed her. She was too hurt to look at him.

Tucking his thumb beneath her chin, he directed her gaze back to him. He was grinning. "Don't be silly, Emily—you'll stay here with me," he explained, obviously able to read her dismay. "You can consider it your own one-night vacation."

"Oh." She felt foolish for having misunderstood Lloyd, but his gentle smile erased her embarrassment.

"I've got to go change into some work clothes," he announced as he started toward the stairway. "I'll be right back."

"Do you want me to come with you?"

He was thoughtful for a moment, then shook his head. "Rest your ankle. I won't be long." Then he vanished up the flight of stairs.

Emily waited, surveying the beautifully decorated parlor. Several antique clocks hung on one wall, a brass cuspidor below them, and a small table across the room from her held an antique pharmacist's scale. An ancient escritoire stood in one corner. She decided that spending a night here, away from her house, away from a place that would only remind her of Gus and feed her worry, was probably a good idea. She would enjoy the change of scenery. Especially since she would be sharing it with Lloyd.

He soon returned to the parlor, clad in weathered jeans and a loose-fitting cotton shirt. "All set," he announced as he helped her off the sofa.

They returned to Emily's house, parked, and headed directly to the backyard, Lloyd toting the chain saw. They lugged the dead tree to a convenient boulder of granite that protruded from the ground and propped one end of the log on it. Emily carefully set a wedge of wood before her legs. Then she yanked the starter cord on the saw, and its motor buzzed to life. "What do you want me to do?" Lloyd asked.

"Hold the log steady," she instructed him. "Keep it from rolling off the rock. It's going to vibrate." He planted his legs on either side of the tilted log, gripped it with his hands, and nodded to Emily that he was ready for her to begin. She set the chained blade against the log and made her first cut.

Several cuts later, Lloyd signaled to her that he was going to release the log, and Emily shut off the saw. "What's wrong?" she asked.

"I want to cut a few," he said, taking the saw from her and studying it intently.

"Have you ever used a chain saw before?" she inquired.

He shook his head.

Emily briefly explained how to start the motor and how to keep the saw from bucking against the log. "Keep this wood here," she warned as she placed the protective wedge in front of his feet. "In case the saw slips—you don't want it landing on your leg."

"I certainly don't," Lloyd agreed. He started the motor, his eyes shining with fascination. As soon as Emily had wedged the dead tree between her knees a safe distance from him, he applied the blade to it.

She watched him as he cut through the trunk, and when the severed section fell free he issued a delighted laugh. "This must be a novelty for a city boy like you," she teased, amazed by the pleasure he derived from what was to her a tedious chore.

He confirmed her supposition with a nod. "It's fun. I always wanted to own a house, to fix it up and work on it the way you do."

Emily smiled but said nothing. She realized that such a dream must have seemed impossible to him once his wife became ill. A woman in a wheelchair would probably have been unable to live comfortably in a house where she might have to contend with stairs or a messy, uneven yard like the one surrounding Emily's cottage.

Emily found herself wondering what other dreams of Lloyd's had gone unfulfilled due to his marriage. Obviously he'd had to defer starting his own business for years, choosing the security of government service over the risks of beginning a new professional venture. She wondered whether he'd wanted children too. Perhaps children, perhaps even a pet dog. His devotion to his wife and her needs would have prevented him from following his own dreams. By the time she'd died he'd lost interest in his dreams to such an extent that the mere mention of them rankled.

The pealing of the telephone's bell through the open kitchen window jolted Emily from her ruminations, and she hollered over the saw's motor that Lloyd should shut it off. Then she hastened to the house with a slight limp, racing through the back door to answer the phone. "Hello?"

"Emily? Tom," her partner said, identifying himself.

She leaned against the counter and tried to catch her breath. "How'd it go?" she asked anxiously.

"As well as could be expected," Tom reported. "I've got his leg pinned together, and he's resting now."

When Tom didn't continue, Emily prodded him. "What's your prognosis, Tom?"

Tom sighed. "He's a fighter, Emily. He won't give up so easily. I'd say the biggest worry right now is the possibility of infection. I've got him all pumped up with antibiotics. I'll come back to the hospital this evening to dose him again."

"I can do that," Emily insisted.

"Emily—"

"Tom, that's the least I can do for him. Come on, let me do that much. I know how to give an injection, for heaven's sake."

"Okay," Tom relented. "He's heavily sedated at the moment. I don't see any need to hang around here all afternoon."

"Of course not. I'll check him this evening."

Tom hesitated, then said, "Emily, that fellow you were with this morning . . ."

"Lloyd?" She hoped Tom wouldn't kid her about her new boyfriend.

"He seems like a nice guy," Tom opined.

"He *is* a nice guy," Emily confirmed.

"Hartford really isn't so far away—"

"That's enough, Tom," Emily interrupted. "I don't need you riding me about him."

"I wasn't going to ride you," Tom defended himself. "I was only going to say that he seems like a nice guy."

"Fine. You've said it," Emily snapped, though she couldn't stifle a tolerant chuckle. "Go home and spend the afternoon with Irene, Tom."

"Will do. Don't worry about Gus, Emily. He's a tough little pup. Well, maybe not little," he contradicted himself. "But tough. He'll be all right."

"Thanks, Tom," Emily said with genuine warmth. "Thanks for everything."

"Forget it. Give me a call if you need anything. Irene and I aren't going anywhere—we'll be home if you need us."

"I appreciate it," Emily asserted. "Take care, Tom."

When she returned to the yard, she found Lloyd leaning against one of the trees from which Gus's runner leash was hung, studying the frayed end of the rope Gus had broken. He looked up immediately at Emily's arrival. "Well?" he asked. "What's the word?"

"He's resting," Emily related. She crossed to Lloyd and wrapped her arms around him, leaning her head against his shoulder. "I'm so glad you're here, Lloyd," she whispered.

Her affectionate gesture seemed to touch him deeply. He closed his arms around her and kissed her brow. "I can't think of anyplace I'd rather be," he murmured. He held her for several silent minutes, then released her. "We should get back to work," he noted.

They spent most of the afternoon cutting up the tree. Emily could have split the sawed chunks of wood with her ax, but since she'd rented the chain saw for the weekend she decided to make use of it, quartering the

circles of wood and stacking them, with Lloyd's assistance, at the rear of her garage. The tree had yielded
enough firewood to see her through a winter month.
Mother Nature had a way of compensating for the
inconveniences she caused—a tree blown into one's
yard could be transformed into a nice supply of free
fuel.

"Why don't you shower and change for dinner?"
Lloyd suggested when the last of the wood was in place.
"Then we can go back to the inn."

"I'll have to detour to the animal hospital first," Emily
told him. "I told Tom I'd check on Gus tonight."

"You can do that in a dress, can't you?"

"Of course," she said as she led Lloyd inside.

He assured her that he'd be able to keep himself
occupied while she washed and dressed, and she left
him in the living room and strode to her bedroom.
Before pulling off her clothes she selected an outfit for
dinner, a gauzy white sundress with a snug bodice and a
flared skirt. Since she couldn't hide the shape of her
body, she chose a dress that would flatter it. Lloyd
claimed to like her figure, with its full bustline and hips,
and the dress made her waist look wonderfully small in
comparison.

She undressed, slipped on her bathrobe, and crossed
to the bathroom to shower. She washed her hair and
blow-dried it, then retaped her ankle. It wasn't bother-
ing her, but she suspected that if she didn't tape it Lloyd
would make a fuss.

Back in her bedroom, she slipped on the dress. The
afternoon had grown muggy, and she decided against
wearing stockings. She stepped into a pair of delicate
sandals that didn't pinch her slightly swollen left foot,
brushed out her hair, and touched her throat with a
fragile scent. For the first time since her divorce, she
wanted to look ravishingly beautiful for a man.

Before leaving her bedroom, she tossed a change of

underwear, a pair of shorts, a cotton shirt, and her hairbrush into a small tote bag. She stopped in the bathroom to add her toothbrush to the bag. Then she sauntered into the living room. It was empty.

She heard a sound coming from the kitchen and she strode to the doorway. Lloyd was on his knees, washing away the bloodstains Gus had left on the linoleum. He glanced up, then smiled and stood, wadding the damp paper towels he'd been using. "Garbage pail?" he asked.

Tears prickling her eyes, Emily waved toward the cabinet beneath the sink. Lloyd swung it open and tossed the paper towels into the pail. He was so sweet, she thought, so helpful, so giving of himself. Her love for him expanded with every new aspect of his personality she discovered, with his every kind action, his every word.

Lloyd straightened up, dusted off his hands, and fixed his gaze upon her, noticing her appearance for the first time and giving her a careful appraisal. His eyebrows rose and his lips shaped an appreciative smile. "Very nice," he complimented her. "Very, very nice." His praise pleased her immensely, and her cheeks colored slightly as she led him to the door.

At his insistence they took his car. He drove straight to the animal hospital and went inside with Emily. She passed through the waiting room and down the back hall to where the spacious cages of overnight patients were housed. She and Tom tried to schedule most surgery at the beginning of the week so their patients could return to their owners by the weekend, and Gus was the only animal spending the night. He lay sleeping on his side in a large, freshly lined cage, a bottle of liquid nutrients attached to the side of the cage with a long tube reaching from it to his mouth in case he wished to drink. His injured leg was enclosed in a thick white plaster cast.

Emily opened the cage's door and brushed her fingers over his nose. It was hot and dry, his breath shallow. "Poor baby," she cooed, running her fingertips between his ears and bending her face as close to his as she could. "Poor Gus. You're going to be all right. You're a fighter, that's what Tom said, and he's right. You're a fighter. You'll pull through."

She withdrew her hand and forced a smile for Lloyd's benefit. "I've got to get some medication," she said as she closed the door of the cage. "I'll be right back." She hurried from the room, gathered up the equipment she needed, and carried it back to Gus. After checking his blood pressure and his pulse, she gave him injections of penicillin and a sedative. "Okay," she sighed to Lloyd after giving Gus a farewell scratch behind his ears. "Let's go."

Lloyd respected her pensive silence as they locked up the building and crossed the lot to his car. He helped her into the car, then gave her hand a gentle squeeze before shutting the door. They didn't speak during the drive to the inn, but as soon as Lloyd had turned off the engine, Emily leaned over and kissed his cheek.

The desk clerk glanced at them as they entered the parlor, her eyes mildly critical. "You look so beautiful, and I look like a bum," Lloyd mumbled to Emily, translating the clerk's disapproving look. "Think you can handle the stairs?"

"If I can't, this evening may turn out to be very disappointing," Emily joked, thoughts of Gus receding as she took heart in Lloyd's strong presence.

He was obviously pleased that her spirits had improved, and he ushered her to the stairs. She leaned on the balustrade and Lloyd slung her arm around his neck, though she could easily have managed the steps without his assistance. She held onto him only because it felt so good to do so.

Upstairs, he escorted her down a corridor to his

room. It was small and cozy, decorated, like the downstairs parlor, with colonial pieces and antiques. The windows, draped with voile curtains, overlooked the lush front lawn of the inn, and the double bed featured a square maple headboard and a handstitched quilt. A rocker stood in one corner, a mirrored bureau against another wall. The floor was covered with an oval braided rug.

While Lloyd unbuttoned his shirt, Emily moved to the window to gaze out at the flowering shrubs below. "I won't be long," Lloyd promised before vanishing into the bathroom. He left the door open, and Emily listened to him showering. Picturing his naked body glistening beneath the spray of water made her blush, an erotic shiver coursing down her spine as she remembered the night they'd spent together and the miracle he'd performed for her. Embarrassed by her imagination, by the way her pulse accelerated when she thought about Lloyd's tender lovemaking, she tried to chase the image from her mind.

Eventually he shut the water, and she heard him at the sink. She stared resolutely at the rhododendron lining the porch beneath the window, hoping her blushing cheeks weren't as vivid a pink as the shrub's blossoms.

At the sound of Lloyd's footsteps entering the bedroom, she spun around. He was moving to the closet, his hair glistening with moisture, his cheeks freshly shaven, a brown towel tied discreetly about his waist. The hair on his chest glittered with residual moisture as well, and Emily sucked in her breath as another dizzying shiver of longing rippled through her.

Lloyd turned to her, his striking eyes sparkling enigmatically. The sheer power in them made her catch her breath. "Anything wrong?" he asked.

"Do—do they offer room service here?" she whispered, shocked by her temerity though she couldn't prevent the words from slipping out.

A smile teased his lips. "I don't think so."

"We could skip dinner."

He took a long step toward Emily. "We could certainly postpone it," he concurred in a dark, husky voice. One more stride carried him to her side, and he coiled his arms around her. His lips came down on hers, firm and eager, and she lifted her hands to his warm, damp shoulders and held him close.

His kiss ignited her body, the now familiar fire of his passion blazing through her. But she felt the tautness too, the coiling of energy in her abdomen that promised far more than fire's mere warmth and light. When Lloyd's mouth left hers to nibble the tip of her nose she gave a shaky laugh. "I can't believe I did that," she murmured.

"Did what? Kissed me?" he asked, leaning back against her hands, savoring their possessive grip on his back.

"Suggested that we skip dinner," she explained. "It's not like me."

"Not like you to skip dinner?"

She knew he was teasing her, and another breathy laugh escaped her. "It's not like me to . . ." She closed her eyes and pressed her head to his chest, oddly bashful. "To want a man so much. I've never felt this way before."

"You make me feel things I've never felt before, too," he growled softly. He ran his hands to her back, locating her dress's zipper and sliding it down. His fingers played briefly across the exposed stretch of skin, and then he pulled the dress from her shoulders, down her arms. As soon as her hands were free of the sleeves, she tugged off his towel.

He hastily finished undressing her and led her to the

bed. They dropped onto it, their arms and legs entwining as they lost themselves in another devouring kiss. Emily felt the tension increasing inside her, coiling, compressing. She tried to relax but she couldn't. She could only trust Lloyd as she'd trusted him last night.

His fingers blazed a path down her, then splayed across her breasts. Her grasp on his back tightened as he hovered above her, caressing the full white flesh that filled his palms. She moaned when his tongue followed the trail of his hands, tasting the crease of her cleavage before detouring to one of her breasts.

The tension continued to build, her body straining against itself. Her hands groped for his hips, mindlessly seeking relief from the poignant ache that twisted through her body to capture her soul. Lloyd shifted, bending his knees, and her fingernails scraped lightly over the backs of his thighs. "Emily," he groaned. "Emily, beautiful woman . . ."

His mouth dipped to her belly, grazing her navel. She clutched his sides, feeling the ridge of his rib cage through his smooth bronze skin. She closed her eyes and felt his weight shifting again. Suddenly her hands gripped not his ribs but his shoulders.

"No," she breathed, not to him but to herself, to the unbelievable sensations his lips imparted to her. *No.* Feelings this magnificent couldn't be real. Emily Squires couldn't be experiencing this. It was impossible. Only a dream.

But if it was a dream, Emily surrendered to the fantasy of it, hurling herself recklessly into the impossible truth of it. Lloyd seemed to sense her approach, her nearness. He swiftly raised himself, binding their bodies together to share the last stretch of the journey together.

Within an instant, it seemed, Lloyd's powerful thrusts pushed her to her limit. She felt the hot shattering inside her, the explosion that burned away the fibers of her body, the dissolving of herself into pulses of energy.

132

She moaned as the exquisite release spread through her, kissing every nerve in her body, every cell.

Lloyd responded to her by increasing the tempo of his thrusts, pushing further, demanding more from her. She was certain she had no more to give him, but she was wrong. His body's motions compelled her onward, forcing the cords to tighten into coils again, tenser than before, harboring more energy. Just as she thought she would go crazy from the pressure, everything sprang loose, consuming her body with a deeper energy, an energy shared by Lloyd as he wrenched free from himself in a shuddering climax.

They didn't speak; they didn't move. For many minutes they just lay together, Lloyd atop Emily, their chests heaving against each other as their lungs struggled for air. At long last Emily's head sank into the pillow and she swallowed. "It happened again," she whispered, incredulous.

Lloyd lifted himself slightly so he could see her. "You didn't think it would?"

"I didn't know," she confessed. "Last night might have been just a fluke."

A bemused smile touched his lips as he studied her. "Emily . . . why didn't you—" He abruptly cut himself off and eased onto the mattress beside her, drawing her to himself and studying the ceiling.

"Why didn't I what?"

He shook his head. "It's none of my business."

"Lloyd." A small giggle escaped her. "By all means, be nosy. I've been so horribly nosy with you, the least you could do is match me in nosiness."

"Nobody could match you in nosiness," Lloyd gently chided her, then grew serious again. He propped himself up on his side and gazed down at her. "How long were you married?"

"Two years," she told him. "I knew my husband for five years before that, though."

"Seven years?" He frowned again. "Seven years, Emily . . . couldn't you and he work it out?"

She knew what Lloyd was referring to, and she turned her head, hiding her face against his chest. She sighed wearily. "Ed didn't think there was anything to work out. He said it was all my fault, I was frigid and defective and only half a woman, and there wasn't anything he could do about it."

She couldn't see Lloyd's face, but she could imagine his frown. He swore softly. "Why did you marry him?"

She opened her mouth and then shut it, pausing to work through her thoughts. "I guess I figured he was right. I mean, we got along well otherwise—at the beginning, anyway—and I didn't know any better. He was more experienced than I was. I figured he knew about these things." She shrugged bitterly. "It couldn't have been his fault. One of the women he was having an affair with thought he was excellent in bed."

Lloyd took a moment to digest her statement. "He told you that?"

"No," Emily said with a wry smile. "She did."

"You met her?"

"Ed introduced us."

Lloyd cursed again. "Why? So she could tell you what an excellent lover he was? So he could get himself off the hook?"

Emily had never even considered that possibility. She mulled it over, then shook her head. "I don't know. Maybe. But the woman would have had no reason to—to get him off the hook. She wasn't after anything more than a quick fling with him. She told me that, too. She was an actress. She had a guest spot on his show for a few weeks, and she told me that as soon as she was done she'd say good-bye to Eddie and move on. She hoped I didn't mind, she said. After all, he was so excellent in bed I certainly shouldn't object to sharing him a little."

Lloyd stared down at her, brushing a lock of hair from her cheek as if by revealing more of her face he'd be able to understand what she was saying. "It sounds . . . kind of perverse," he managed.

"It was just the way things were there, Lloyd," she reminded him. "Everybody let it all hang out. Ed introduced me to another woman he was having an affair with, too. At a party. She also commented that Ed knew his stuff."

Lloyd grimaced. "What did you do?"

"I filed for divorce," Emily replied simply.

Lloyd nodded at the abundant sensibility of Emily's decision. He continued to stroke her hair back from her face, his eyes silvery, his thoughts hidden until he spoke. "So you believed there was something wrong with you."

"What else should I have believed?" Emily challenged him. "Ed was obviously capable of satisfying half of Los Angeles County, based on a random sampling of two."

"Emily." His lips flexed as he contemplated his words before speaking. "Even if these women were telling the truth about your husband, it doesn't make him a good lover. No two women are alike."

"I take it you're speaking from experience?" Emily affectionately teased him.

He examined her face to make certain that there was nothing condemning in her attitude. "I was twenty-six when I got married," he informed her. "And I've been widowed for five years. I've known a few women." He reflected for a moment. "The women I've met since my wife died . . ." He smiled pensively. "None of them responded to me the way you do."

Emily was flabbergasted. Lloyd was so sensitive, so generous a lover—she couldn't believe that they wouldn't have responded to him. She opened her mouth to protest, but he continued before she had a chance. "I don't mean physically, Emily, I mean emotionally. You're the most open, honest woman I've ever met. The bravest. The strongest. I might have satisfied other women, but . . . but they seemed to be satisfied with much less. Not just physically but emotionally. You demand a lot, Emily, more than I thought I could ever give. But you earn it. You deserve it."

Emily fought to understand his words. She knew they came from his heart. Perhaps she had demanded too much from Lloyd. Yet he'd given her everything she'd asked for, and more.

"You did love your wife, didn't you?" she whispered.

He nestled his head against the pillow, his eyes never leaving Emily. "Yes," he admitted.

"Tell me about her," she entreated him. "What was her name?"

"Diane."

"What did she look like?"

Lloyd accepted Emily's inquiry without flinching. Once again she was demanding things from him, and once again he seemed to feel she deserved what she was demanding. "She was small. Petite. We probably looked funny together, like Mutt and Jeff." He smiled hesitantly, and Emily smiled as well. "Dark coloring, dark eyes. She was very athletic. I think that made her condition harder for her to bear. She was a fantastic tennis player."

"Better than me, huh?"

He nodded. "Better than me."

"What did she do?"

He puzzled over the question. "Professionally, you mean?" At Emily's confirming nod, he sighed. "Nothing. She came from a wealthy family. Her greatest aspiration was to get married. I used to think sometimes that if she'd had a career, something to occupy her mind, she wouldn't have been so devastated by what happened to her body. Many victims of MS live with the disease for years and years. It's a matter of one's state of mind, I think. Diane had nothing but tennis and golf. When she lost those, she had nothing."

"She had you," Emily murmured.

Lloyd mused for a moment. "Apparently that wasn't enough."

Emily cuddled closer to Lloyd, her head cushioned by his upper arm. "I wish . . ." Her voice drifted off.

"You wish what?" He urged her to continue.

"I wish I'd known you then. I wish I could have helped you through it the way you've helped me today. That sounds insane, doesn't it?" she laughed softly. "I don't mean I wish I knew you like *this*"—her hand brushed lovingly over his chest—"but as a friend, Lloyd, someone to offer support when you needed it. I wish I could have done that for you."

"You have, Emily," he murmured. "You have done that for me."

She lapsed into silence. Lloyd had answered questions she hadn't even asked, and she didn't need to say anything more.

8

He left after breakfast on Sunday. It was a drizzly, overcast day, so they couldn't go swimming or boating. The rain suited Emily; even if the weather had been fair, she wanted only to return to the animal hospital to spend the day with Gus. After promising to call her that evening, Lloyd tactfully chose to leave so she could attend to her pet.

She remained by Gus's side for most of the afternoon, injecting him with antibiotics, stroking him, talking to him, forcing liquid nourishment down his throat with an oversized pipette tube. Occasionally Gus would open his bleary eyes, but they didn't focus on Emily. Then he would groan feebly and drift into unconsciousness again. There really wasn't much Emily could do for him, but merely sitting beside his cage, whispering words of encouragement and caressing his motionless body, made her feel better.

By Monday, Emily's ankle had shrunk back to its

normal size, but Gus had shown no improvement. At least his condition hadn't worsened, Tom pointed out optimistically, but Emily wasn't comforted. She spent every spare minute in the back room ministering to Gus—and some minutes that weren't spare. "We've got a waiting room crowded with howling critters," Sally scolded her once when she found Emily moping by Gus's cage. "Shake a leg, would you? Standing here and wringing your hands won't do him one bit of good."

Emily nodded and returned to her office. Sally was right, she sighed as she apathetically examined a beagle pup and gave it its first set of vaccinations. Fretting wasn't going to help Gus. If he was going to fight off the fever that tormented him, regain his strength, and knit his leg, he would do it whether or not Emily hovered over his cage. Yet her feeling of relative uselessness was agonizing, and as soon as she issued a clean bill of health to the puppy, she raced back to Gus's cage to watch him sleep.

"I hope you won't be insulted," Tom commented as he and Emily closed up for the day, "but you were really awful to be around today."

"I know," she lamented. "I'm sorry."

"You aren't accomplishing anything by clinging to the bars of his cage and eating your heart out," he reminded her.

"I know, Tom, I know. I didn't pull my weight today, and I've been in a wretched mood, and you and Sally are wonderful to put up with me. I'll try to be cheerier tomorrow."

Tom shut and locked the front door, then took Emily's arm and steered her across the lot to her station wagon. "I've got a better idea," he suggested. "Don't come in tomorrow. Take a day off and unwind."

"I couldn't!" Emily protested.

"Sure you can take a day off."

"I couldn't unwind," she clarified with a doleful laugh. "Tom, if I hang around my house all day I'll only feel worse. I'll stand at the window staring at Gus's runner leash and hating myself for not having bought a stronger leash before it was too late." Tom turned her to face him, and her dark eyes glistened imploringly. "Please let me come in and keep busy. I'll be better—I promise."

Tom's lips twisted in a dubious scowl, but he relented. "Okay. I'll see you tomorrow," he said before swinging her car's door open for her.

Emily broke her promise; by Tuesday she was, if anything, more insufferably gloomy. Gus had deteriorated slightly overnight; his fever had risen and he refused to swallow the fluid Emily forced into his mouth when she arrived at the clinic. She tried to contain her anguish, but she couldn't. She was distracted, distraught, barely able to concentrate on her other patients. At three o'clock Tom stormed into her office. "Get out," he ordered.

"What?" She glanced up from her file on a recently spayed cat who had just had its postoperative checkup.

"Get out. Go home. I can't stand looking at you anymore."

His gentle tone belied the harshness of his words, and Emily forced a feeble smile to her lips. "We don't close for another two hours," she pointed out.

Tom approached her, his eyes studying her intensely. "When was the last time you got any sleep?"

"Last night," she lied.

He shook his head in disbelief. "Go home," he murmured. "Do us all a favor. Do Gus a favor and take off for a few days. We don't have such a heavy schedule this week. Get away for a while, would you?"

She sighed. "I'm that bad, am I?"

"You're that bad," Tom confirmed sympathetically.

Emily sighed, then rose and pulled off her white coat. "Far be it from me to argue with you, Dr. Henderson," she muttered. "I'll take off the rest of the afternoon."

"And tomorrow," Tom commanded.

Eyeing him with obvious irritation, she closed the cat's file and inserted it into the file cabinet behind her desk. "Let's take this one day at a time, shall we?"

"Fair enough." Tom gave her a friendly hug, then handed her her purse and nudged her out of the office. He escorted her to the front door, unwilling to give her a chance to change her mind, and as soon as she was outside he called, "See you next week." He slammed the door on her before she could contradict him.

Not knowing what else to do, she drove home. After tossing her purse onto the kitchen table, she filled a glass with milk and carried it outside to her porch. In addition to not sleeping well, she hadn't been eating. Without conscious effort, she'd lost a couple of pounds, but she wasn't particularly happy about it. She sipped her milk and hoped it would compensate for the breakfast and lunch she'd skipped.

The ringing of the telephone roused her, and she went indoors to answer it. Probably Tom was calling her, she decided with a self-righteous sniff, begging her to return to work. If he hadn't desperately needed a partner, he wouldn't have asked her to buy into the animal hospital, would he? She lifted the receiver. "Hello."

"Hello, Emily," said Lloyd.

"Lloyd!" She didn't bother to conceal her surprise. She'd spoken to him Sunday night and again Monday night, and he'd told her he'd phone in the evening on Tuesday. She hadn't expected him to call in the middle of the afternoon. "Aren't you at work?"

He laughed. "I've got a telephone at work," he playfully informed her. "Indoor plumbing too. Just like Kansas."

His joke buoyed her spirits. As depressing as her crisis with Gus was, she couldn't deny the joy merely thinking of Lloyd brought her. "So you're at work," she said. "Didn't you assume I'd be at work, too?"

He paused. "But you aren't," he pointed out.

"Come on, Lloyd," she pressed him suspiciously. "Why did you try me at home?"

"I've just been talking to Tom," Lloyd confessed. "He told me you'd left the clinic."

Emily was bewildered. "You said you'd call me in the evening. Why did you try to reach me during the day?"

"I didn't," Lloyd admitted. "I wanted to talk to Tom. You keep telling me you're doing all right, but you sound ghastly, Emily. I called Tom and he told me you're a wreck."

"Wonderful," she groaned. "What else did he tell you?"

"He told me he wants you to take some time off from work," Lloyd reported. "That sounds like a good idea to me."

"Good God," Emily complained. "The two people in the world I thought I could trust are gossiping about me behind my back—"

"Emily." Lloyd sounded stern. "He's right. You need to get away from Gus." He hesitated, and when he next spoke his voice was soft and cajoling. "Why don't you spend the rest of the week with me here in Hartford?"

"What?"

"Come to Hartford," he repeated. "Spend the week with me."

The invitation was tempting, but she resisted it. "Just because I let Tom talk me into taking a couple of hours off today doesn't mean I'm quitting my job. I've got an animal hospital to run here, Lloyd. I can't take the entire week off."

"Who's being a workaholic now?" Lloyd argued.

"Tom assured me he can survive without you for a few days. In fact, he swore he'd get much more work done if he didn't have to worry about you."

"He doesn't have to worry about me," Emily snapped. "I'm not a wreck, no matter what he says."

But she was, and Lloyd knew it. "Come to Hartford," he persisted. "Come be with me."

She felt herself weakening. "What'll I do while you're at work?"

"You'll rest and relax," Lloyd recommended.

Emily realized that Tom must have provided Lloyd with an in-depth report on her condition. As much as she resented the idea of Tom and Lloyd in cahoots, plotting to spirit her away from her work for some well-needed rest, she appreciated their thoughtfulness and concern. She let out her breath in a low sigh. "All right," she conceded. "I'll come."

"I'll be home from work by five-thirty," Lloyd assured her brightly. "Let me give you directions." He waited for Emily to find a pencil and some paper, then provided her with directions to his home. "It's about an hour's drive," he concluded. "I can tell the superintendent and arrange to have him let you in if you get there before me."

"That's all right," Emily declined. "I'll wait until four-thirty to leave."

"I'll see you tonight then," Lloyd said. "Take care."

After bidding him good-bye, Emily hung up. She honestly wasn't angry, either with Tom or with Lloyd. That they cared enough about her to conspire behind her back flattered her a great deal.

She packed a bag with enough clothing to last her through the weekend, and at four-thirty she locked up her house and embarked on her drive to Hartford. Lloyd's directions were accurate, and she had no difficulty finding his address, a modern high-rise complex on the outskirts of Hartford. She parked in a space marked for visitors near the front door of Lloyd's building and noticed his black BMW parked in a reserved space across the lot, indicating that he'd already arrived home from his office. The doorman signaled Lloyd on the building's intercom and then pointed her in the direction of the elevator.

The building's lobby was chic and modern, the elevator glaringly lit. She got out on Lloyd's floor and toted her suitcase down the long corridor to his door. He opened it before she could ring.

Seeing him elated Emily. His smile as he swept her into the apartment's foyer proved his delight at seeing her as well. His eyes looked beautiful to her, a gentle, luminous blue. He gathered her into his powerful arms and held her tightly. "Thank you for coming," he murmured.

"Thank you for talking me into it," Emily whispered, pressing her cheek to the lapel of the dark gray business suit he wore. She noticed that his striped tie was loosened and his collar unbuttoned. Evidently he'd just returned home.

Leaving one arm firmly wrapped around her shoulders, he hoisted her suitcase and led her into the living room. Emily surveyed the room and suffered a twinge of shock at its starkness. The furniture consisted of austere couches and chairs of gray leather that somehow looked drab to her, and plain parsons tables. The white walls were devoid of artwork, the tops of the tables and sideboard were empty, the carpet a pristine beige. The room seemed sterile, untouched by human warmth.

Lloyd seemed oblivious to her surprise. "Let me change my clothes, and then we'll have some supper, all right?" he said as he carried her suitcase through the living room to a hallway. Emily tried to shake off her discomfort with the unadorned living room as she followed him to his bedroom.

It bore the same chilliness, its furnishings austere, its colors muted, its walls and windowsills barren. "You don't like art?" she blurted out as Lloyd set down the suitcase and shrugged off his jacket.

He was halfway to his walk-in closet before her comment sank in. "Art?" he asked, bewildered.

"I mean—a painting on the walls or something," she faltered, not wishing to sound critical. "Some posters, maybe . . ."

He meditated for a moment, then reached for a suit hanger. "I never thought about it," he allowed. "You don't like the apartment?"

"Well, it's . . ." She bit her lip, then forced out the truth. "It's got about as much personality as a motel room."

"Hmm." He didn't seem to be insulted, only thoughtful as he kicked off his loafers and placed them neatly on the floor of the closet. "It's where I live," he murmured. "I've never given much thought to fixing it up beyond that."

She wondered briefly whether he considered dressing up one's home a woman's responsibility. Then she discarded that notion. Lloyd's comment over the weekend about his dream of owning a house that he could work on implied that he would take pleasure in marking his home with his own personality. Maybe he didn't consider his apartment a home; he said it was simply the place where he lived. Maybe he'd abandoned his dream of a *real* home long ago.

That possibility saddened Emily, but as he removed the trousers of his suit her sadness ebbed, replaced by the utter delight of seeing his long, well-proportioned legs. A wild yearning shot through her at the sight, and she struggled to hide her disappointment when he stepped into a pair of jeans and pulled them up. He carefully arranged the creases of the suit's trousers on the hanger, then glanced up, reading Emily's undeniably lustful expression. His smile reflected a blend of amusement, mischief, and pleasure. "I'm very glad you came," he whispered.

Emily felt her cheeks grow hot, but she courageously met his gaze. "I'm glad I came, too," she admitted softly.

Their conversation over dinner was casual. Diplomatically, Lloyd didn't ask about Gus. Instead he described a report his firm was preparing on mortgage rate fluctuations for one of the state's investment companies. Emily tried to follow his discourse on the data manipulations and guesswork involved in forecasting economic trends, but it struck her as terribly esoteric work. She was intelligent and well-educated, yet Lloyd's description of his project left her slightly dazed. So she mostly listened and ate. For the first time in days, she managed to consume an entire nutritionally balanced meal. She proudly admired her empty plate and decided that if her mother could see her now she'd have no cause to bemoan Emily's unwitting contribution to the starvation of Asian children.

After dinner Emily and Lloyd retired to bed. Lloyd's glorious lovemaking couldn't alter Gus's condition, but it altered Emily's, replenishing her reserves of strength and confidence. Usually so forthright, Emily found herself unable to express in words the ecstasy Lloyd had liberated within her—not just the physical ecstasy of their sexual compatibility but the emotional ecstasy of knowing that she was a complete, responsive woman. She wanted to give voice to her joy, but words seemed inadequate. Yet when she saw her joy mirrored in Lloyd's eyes she knew words weren't necessary.

They rose early, and after Lloyd had dressed for work

and they'd consumed a light breakfast, he gave her a spare set of keys and drew her a small map illustrating the simplest route from his home to his office. "Come by around noon and we'll have lunch together," he suggested. "I've got a busy day, so I can't promise you more than an hour."

"An hour will do," she accepted. "I'll be there at twelve."

Once he had gone she showered and dressed in a white cotton blouse and a flowered A-line skirt. Then she telephoned Tom at the animal hospital. He briskly informed her that Gus was doing as well as could be expected and that she should stop worrying about him. She expressed concern about stranding Tom with a full schedule, but he insisted that he and Sally could handle the load without her, and that she should relax and put thoughts of sick animals out of her mind for a few days. He terminated the hurried call with the observation that, while he wasn't overworked, he *was* busy, and Emily bade him good-bye.

Restless, wishing she could take Tom's advice and stop worrying, Emily prowled through Lloyd's apartment. She still felt unnerved by its austerity. Just a painting, a few knickknacks, *something* to brighten the place up would make such a difference, she thought. His apartment put her in mind of a mausoleum, a place where he had buried himself to grieve for his wife and his marriage. The rooms seemed as cold to her as Lloyd's eyes had been when she'd first met him. But Lloyd's eyes had changed in the weeks Emily had known him. They were soft and animated now, brimming with life. Perhaps in time he would be ready to liven up his home as well.

She wandered into his den, the only room in the apartment that appeared at all lived in. It held a reclining chair and an overstuffed sofa, a television set, and a wall of built-in bookcases. Emily combed the shelves in search of something to read. Her lip reflexively curled in distaste as she studied his library. Most of the books were hardcover volumes dealing with economics or history; his meager fiction collection consisted of the complete works of Henry James bound in leather along one shelf, the epics of Homer, and a sampling of novels by Disraeli, Dickens, and Thackeray. Not a single entertaining bestseller among them.

She pulled a book about industrial management from a shelf and leafed through it. Although the subject didn't interest her, Emily found the book more or less readable, and she perused several chapters before leaving the apartment to meet Lloyd for lunch. She drove into downtown Hartford, losing her way only once as she navigated the crowded streets that had been taken over in the past several decades by exotic modern skyscrapers. Eventually she located Lloyd's building and parked in its underground garage. Then she rode the elevator up to the floor that contained his office. She easily located the door marked LLOYD GORDON ASSOCIATES and entered.

A pretty young receptionist greeted her with an impassive smile. "May I help you?" she asked.

"I'm here to see Lloyd Gordon," Emily announced. "My name is Emily Squires."

"Please be seated." The receptionist gestured to a low-slung leather couch across the reception area from her desk. Emily scanned the room before sitting. The couch and matching chairs were as functional and uninspiring as the furniture in Lloyd's apartment, and the white walls were devoid of decoration.

Taking a seat, she watched the receptionist lift a telephone and push a button. "I'm sorry to bother you, Mr. Gordon," she apologized, her green eyes riveted on Emily as she spoke. "A woman named Emily Squires is here to see you." The receptionist listened for a moment, then replaced the receiver. "He'll be with you in a few minutes," she said.

Emily smiled politely and lifted an issue of *Business Week* from the coffee table before her. She flipped uninterestedly through it, then dropped it back to the table. The receptionist was staring at her with curiosity. Emily smiled again, mildly uneasy under the young woman's blatant scrutiny of her.

At last she heard activity in the hall leading out of the reception area. The sound of men's voices preceded the arrival into the entry area of Lloyd and an older, silver-haired man wearing a conservative business suit. Lloyd glimpsed Emily and winked, then turned his attention back to the man. "We'll have something for you by the end of the month," he informed his client. "I'll be in touch if we need more information."

The older man shook Lloyd's hand and thanked him, and Lloyd opened the door leading from the office suite. Once the man was gone, Lloyd turned and moved directly to Emily. "I'm sorry we ran late," he whispered. "He's kind of a pompous windbag. I couldn't get him to shut up."

Emily grinned. "If you're busy, Lloyd, we can skip lunch."

"Not a chance." He took her hand to help her up from the sofa, then immediately released her, keeping a discreet distance between them. "I'm taking lunch out today," he told the receptionist. "I'll be back in an hour."

The receptionist eyed Emily inquisitively but said nothing. Her gaze remained on them as they left the office. Not until they reached the elevator did Lloyd kiss Emily's cheek. "Why was she gawking at me like that?" Emily asked as Lloyd wove his fingers through hers.

"Was she gawking at you?" Lloyd asked, glancing over his shoulder in the direction of his office. The elevator arrived, and he shrugged as he ushered Emily into the car. "I don't usually take women out to lunch," he explained. "In fact, the only women I take out to lunch are clients. She knew you weren't a client."

Emily ran her eyes over her outfit. "I'm not dressed for the part, huh?"

Lloyd chuckled. "Connie knows my schedule backward and forward. She knew I didn't have a business lunch planned." He squeezed Emily's hand, then released it. "As a rule I conduct my social life far away from the office," he explained.

"Are you sorry I came to your office?"

He peered down at her, his eyes twinkling. "Of course not. If I didn't want you to come I wouldn't have asked you." The elevator opened onto the lobby, and they left the building.

Emily didn't question Lloyd further. That he had permitted her to invade his office—that he'd chosen to go public with her—pleased her. Emily knew how reserved and private Lloyd was. His willingness to reveal his relationship with her to his colleagues implied an openness and a commitment that thrilled her.

They strolled to a nearby coffee shop. Once they'd ordered sandwiches, Lloyd leaned back in his chair and smiled at Emily. He looked so handsome, his eyes as remarkably vivid in color as they were, complemented by the navy blue wool of his suit, that Emily couldn't resist returning his smile. "What have you been doing with yourself all morning?" he asked.

"I called Tom," she told him.

His brows arched slightly. "And what did he have to say?"

"He said I should stop worrying," Emily mumbled.

"Sounds like good advice." The waitress deposited their sandwiches and drinks on the table. Lloyd took a sip of his iced tea, then asked, "What else did you do?"

"I read a little. Lloyd, you have the worst collection of books I've ever seen!"

"What's wrong with my books?" he asked, slightly offended.

She swallowed a bite of her sandwich before groaning, "Henry James? Honestly, Lloyd, *nobody* reads Henry James. Nobody but college freshmen stuck in required literature survey courses."

Lloyd laughed. "Henry James is an excellent stylist," he said defending the author.

"Henry James is a worse pompous windbag than the guy you were meeting with before lunch. Who reads a novel because of the style?" She shook her head, then took another bite of her sandwich. "Give me a good plot and a few interesting characters—that's what I want in a novel. Not style." Her grimace evoked an amused chuckle from Lloyd.

They chatted about inconsequential things for the remainder of their lunch, and when Lloyd checked his watch he winced. "I've got to run," he muttered. "Jam-packed afternoon."

He hastily settled the bill and they left the restaurant. They walked hand in hand back to his building and parted ways in the lobby, Lloyd to return to his office and Emily to fetch her car. She studied the diagram he'd drawn for her and wended her way through the traffic toward his apartment.

Not far from the complex, she spotted a small shopping center, and she impulsively steered into its parking lot, searching for a store where she might be able to buy some books more interesting than Henry James novels or treatises on management theory. A large discount department store anchored one end of the shopping center, and Emily parked and entered the building.

Before she could reach the paperback book section, she noticed a display of houseplants for sale. Forgetting her original purpose in visiting the store, she wandered up and down the aisles of the plant department. Lloyd's apartment needed plants. They would surely liven the place up.

After lengthy deliberation, she chose a philodendron, a prayer plant, and a passion plant. She carefully balanced the plants in her arms and lugged them to the cashier, who helpfully gave her a cardboard carton in which to carry them. Emily paid for them and returned to Lloyd's apartment. The doorman eyed her carton quizzically but said nothing as she nodded a greeting and headed for the elevator.

When she reached Lloyd's apartment, she locked the door behind her and set down the carton. She surveyed the living room and decided to put the plants along the windowsill. Lloyd could place them elsewhere if he wished. Once the three plants were lined up beneath the window, Emily stepped back to gauge the effect. A definite improvement, she opined. The apartment was one small step closer to being a home.

She roamed to the den, lifted the book she'd been reading, and arranged herself comfortably on the recliner. The book's boring subject matter had a tranquilizing effect on her, especially given the insomnia she'd been suffering the past several nights, and after reading several pages she nodded off.

She was still napping when Lloyd arrived home; she didn't even hear him enter the den. He clasped her shoulders and shook them gently, and when she opened her eyes her vision filled with the glorious sight of him. She smiled.

Lloyd smiled too, then grew solemn. "What did you do?"

"I conked out," Emily mumbled groggily, rolling her head from shoulder to shoulder to loosen the muscles of her neck. She lifted the open book from her lap. "Real exciting literature you've got here, Lloyd. More effective than sleeping pills."

He waited for her to set the book aside and rise

before he spoke again. "I meant in the living room. Where did those plants come from?"

"Oh—do you like them?" Emily asked gleefully as she led him from the den. He loosened his tie as he joined her in the living room. "They're beautiful, aren't they? They add a bit of color to the room. I think they look great. Maybe you want to rearrange them—"

"Emily, if I wanted plants all over the house, I would have bought some myself."

His dry tone derailed her enthusiasm. She turned from the window to find him staring distastefully at the greenery. "You don't like plants?" she asked in a small voice.

"I don't want them all over my living room."

"They're not all over your living room," she pointed out. "They're on your windowsill."

He crossed to the sill, his lips pressed grimly together, his eyes icing over. "So they're on my windowsill," he muttered. "How do I get rid of them?"

"You don't," she asserted, matching him in forcefulness. "You water them and talk to them and enjoy them. And they grow, and then you enjoy them even more. The prayer plant needs more water than the other two—once or twice a week for the philodendron and passion plant, maybe three times a week for the prayer plant. But you don't want to drown them, just moisten the soil. Unless they look droopy or start to lose their leaves—"

"Emily." He exhaled, then confronted her. "The last thing I want in my life is to have to be nursing a bunch of plants. I don't want to have to be fidgeting with their soil and inspecting their leaves and watching them shrivel up and die all over the carpet."

"They won't shrivel up if you take good care of them," she claimed.

"I don't want to take care of them." Lloyd's voice was hoarse and clipped. "Don't you understand? Even if I take good care of them they might just shrivel up and die on me. *I don't want them.*"

His eyes were glacial, his mouth tense. A miserable ache gripped Emily's stomach as she stared into his face and comprehended the pain in its grim lines. It wasn't the plants that he didn't want, but the caring for them, the nurturing of them, the responsibility of keeping them alive. He had done enough nursing to last a lifetime, as he'd told her—and even his devoted effort hadn't prevented his wife from shriveling up and dying on him.

Her heart swelled with pity. Not pity for the sorrow he'd endured in losing his wife, but pity for his refusal to overcome it. "Lloyd," she murmured, her tone gentle but unshakable. "These are plants, not people. If they die, it's ten dollars down the drain. And if they thrive, it's—it's the difference between a home that feels like a home and a home that feels like a—a tomb."

"A tomb?" Her choice of that word made him recoil slightly. She saw his eyes growing colder as he retreated from her.

"Yes," she bravely insisted. "A tomb. If you're really tired of eating yourself up, if you really want to get it all out of your system, then start with some plants." Her voice softened and she dared to approach him. She curled her fingers around his elbow and led him to the plants. "Just a little water twice a week. They won't die."

He gazed dubiously at the plants, then reached out to touch the exotic purple fuzz coating the dark green leaves of the passion plant. "What if they do?" he asked hesitantly.

She rose on tiptoe and kissed his lips. "Lloyd, don't you know what you're capable of?" She kissed him again, peering into his eyes, silently begging them to thaw. "You can't kill these plants. If they die, it's because they were meant to die—they weren't hearty enough or strong enough. And if they live, it's because you gave them the chance to live."

"That's an interesting explanation," Lloyd grunted skeptically. "Either way I come out the hero."

"That's right," Emily said. "That's the way it works."

He tore his eyes from the plants and let them flood her face with their metallic light. They still seemed cold to Emily, glinting with doubt. "What makes you think I'm capable of taking care of them?"

"I know what you've done for me," she breathed.

Slowly his arms wound around her and he drew her snugly to him. His lips browsed through her hair and then he rested his chin on the crown of her lowered head. "What do I do with them if I want to take a vacation?"

She smiled, as much at the strange sensation of his jaw moving against her skull as at his words. "Depends on how long the vacation is going to be," she replied, her voice slightly muffled by his chest. "More than a couple of weeks, you can ask a neighbor to water them for you. Less than that, you can soak the soil, put a plastic bag around each plant, and keep your fingers crossed."

"How about just a few days?"

She twisted out of his grip and raised her eyes to him. "What did you have in mind?"

"We're going away tomorrow."

Emily's brows knitted in a frown. "What are you talking about?"

"A fellow I know through work is lending us a cottage he owns on Cape Cod for a couple of days. I picked up the keys on my way home today. We're leaving tomorrow."

"Tomorrow?" Her frown deepened. "What about your work?"

"If you aren't going to be a workaholic, why should

155

I?" he posed, releasing her and drifting across the room, sliding off his blazer. "It's hard for me to concentrate when I know you're here all alone, rattling around and being bored. I thought it would do us both some good to get away."

She tried to decipher the undercurrent in his words. It didn't seem like Lloyd just to run off for a few days. It had taken him five years to indulge in a vacation, and that vacation had cost him no time away from his office. And it had in reality been less a vacation than an attempt to exorcise his past. "Lloyd." She took a step toward him and he turned back to face her, his eyes now exquisitely tender and warm. "Lloyd, why do you want to get away?"

"To be with you, just the two of us." He came closer, then gathered her into his arms. "All right?"

"All right." She didn't have to think; the words sprang from her heart. She could never refuse such an unexpectedly romantic invitation from the man she loved. Of course she would go away with him, just the two of them, for as long as he wanted. She would gladly go away with him forever, and if the plants shriveled up and died she wouldn't care at all.

9

∞∞∞∞∞∞∞∞∞

I didn't bring a swimsuit," Emily remarked.

"You won't need one," Lloyd assured her. "According to Glenn, the water's too cold to swim in until mid-July."

"Have you ever been to Cape Cod?" Emily asked.

It was eight A.M., and they'd already been on the road for an hour. Lloyd had insisted on getting an early start, since they had a four-hour-plus trip ahead of them. Emily hadn't bothered telephoning Tom to get an update on Gus's condition before they left. She figured she'd give the animal hospital a call once she and Lloyd were settled in at the cottage Lloyd's friend had lent them for the weekend.

In answer to her question he shook his head.

"Where did you take vacations when you were a child?" Emily asked.

"Fire Island. My parents had a summer home there."

"You must have been rich," Emily mused. "The rich kid in town, as you'd say."

Lloyd chuckled. "I guess we were. We were comfortable, and if you live in Manhattan, you've got to be rich to be comfortable." He shrugged. "To me, rich kids were kids who lived in houses. Kids who had their own backyards."

"You must have had a yard on Fire Island," Emily commented. At Lloyd's confirming nod, she asked, "Do your folks still have a home there?"

"No, they sold it when I left for college."

"Raising money so they could afford to send you to Yale?" she teased.

He laughed again. "They were already thinking about retirement by the time I was out of my teens. They spent a few years shopping around for a place in a warmer climate to retire to. About eight years ago they moved to Bermuda."

"Bermuda!" Emily sighed. "How lovely. Do you visit them often?" Lloyd shook his head again, and Emily remembered that he didn't take vacations. She settled into her bucket seat and did a quick calculation. "Eight years ago," she pondered. That would have been while Lloyd was still married. "Didn't they—?" She bit her lip to stifle her words.

He shot her a quick glance, then turned his attention back to the road. "Go ahead, be nosy," he permitted.

"It's just—I would have thought they'd want to stay close to you. Given what you were going through with your wife eight years ago."

Lloyd reminisced for a moment, then sighed. "I didn't want them close by," he admitted. "I sort of pushed them into making the move."

"Why?"

"They were awful to be around," he explained pensively. "My father would look at Diane and his eyes would fill with tears. My mother was just the opposite—

she was the brainless optimist, prattling on about how next year Diane would be on her feet again, playing tennis. It was unbearable. I told them to move away, to get out of our hair." He pressed his lips together, lost for a moment in thought. "They were hurt that I didn't want their help. I think they still are, a little. We've only recently begun to work it out."

Emily nodded sympathetically. "What about your wife's parents? Were they any better?"

Lloyd fell silent, concentrating on a sluggish truck he wanted to pass. Once he was back in the right-hand lane he addressed Emily's question. "Her father died before I met her. Her mother . . . her mother hated me."

Emily's jaw dropped. She couldn't imagine why any woman would hate a man like Lloyd, who had willingly dedicated himself to the care of her daughter. "How could she hate you?"

"She associated Diane's illness with me. She irrationally decided it was my fault. She never passed up an opportunity to remind me that Diane had never been sick a day in her life until I married her." He exhaled again, his mouth grim and his eyes steely. "After her visits, I'd feel the repercussions for weeks. I think she managed to convince Diane every time she saw her that I was to blame for what had happened."

Emily reached across the stick shift and squeezed Lloyd's arm consolingly. "I'm sure your mother-in-law didn't mean it. She was probably only doing a lousy job of handling her own grief."

Lloyd eyed Emily thoughtfully, and his expression softened. "You're right," he mused. "At the time it was hard not to take it personally, but you're right." He drifted into wistful meditation for a while, then smiled. "How about you? Where did your family take vacations?"

"Nowhere exciting," she grumbled good-naturedly.

"The Ozarks, Yellowstone Park, places like that. I didn't see the ocean until I was in college." She grinned. "When you're growing up in Kansas, the ocean seems as far away as Paris, and about as alien. My father always drew the biggest crowds to his movies when he rented beach-party films. We used to study them as if they were travelogues. Who cared that the plots were silly? We'd all just sit there and gape at the beach scenes. I mean, surf! We couldn't believe the movies were filmed on the planet earth, let alone in our own country." Lloyd joined her laughter.

They reached the cottage shortly before noon. It was more a ramshackle cabin than a house, one of a small cluster of cabins on a dirt road in Dennis Port, a village on the southern shore of the Cape. They unloaded their bags from the trunk of the car and Lloyd unlocked the cabin's door.

It was as dilapidated inside as out. The floor of the minuscule living room listed slightly, and the kitchen was barely the size of a closet. The two bedrooms each contained single beds, and the bathroom was so tiny that a person had to slide past the sink sideways to reach the stall shower. "There's no telephone," Emily complained after searching the four rooms.

Lloyd twisted the kitchen sink's faucet, and a trickle of water emerged from the tap. "But there's indoor plumbing," he declared. "Just like Kansas."

Emily allowed herself a slight smile before growing serious. "Lloyd, I've got to call Tom."

Lloyd glanced at her, then turned away, rummaging through the kitchen's few cabinets, which contained pots, dishes, and utensils, but no food. "You don't *have* to call him," he pointed out.

"Of course I do. I want to find out how Gus is faring."

Lloyd closed the door of the broom closet and pivoted to face Emily. "Whether or not you call Tom isn't going to make any difference in Gus's condition, you know. Why don't you just relax and have faith in Tom? He's doing what's best for the dog."

Emily nodded at Lloyd's sensibility, but she wasn't satisfied. "I know he's doing what's best for Gus, but I still want to talk to him." She surveyed the kitchen. "We've got to go into town to pick up some food. I'll call him from a phone booth."

"If you want," Lloyd conceded with a sigh.

As soon as they'd unpacked their bags in one of the bedrooms, they drove to the main boulevard running through Dennis Port and cruised it until they found a supermarket. Before Emily could consider shopping, she scouted out a telephone booth outside the store and raced to it. Lloyd patiently followed her, loitering beside the booth's door.

Rather than feeding several dollars' worth of coins into the phone, Emily telephoned the animal hospital collect. Sally accepted the call, and as soon as the operator was off the line she accosted Emily. "For heaven's sake, Emily—why are you calling collect?"

"For heaven's sake yourself, Sally," Emily mocked her. "When you get the phone bill, you can deduct the cost of this call from my pay check."

"In that case, let's save you some money and be brief," Sally stated. "As it is, I haven't got time to shoot the breeze with you. The waiting room is teeming with patients."

Emily cringed. "I shouldn't have gone away and left you and Tom alone. I knew we'd be busy this week—"

"I didn't mean that," Sally hastily amended. "We can handle things here just fine, Emily. No problem."

Emily thought Sally was lying, but she appreciated her attempt to reassure her. "Is Tom around?" she asked.

"He's doing a spay right now," Sally reported.

"How's Gus?"

"Don't worry about Gus," Sally said swiftly. "Honestly, Emily, you don't have to keep checking up on us. We know what to do for him. You don't have to badger us to death. I mean," she added rapidly, "we're doing what's best for him. You know we are."

Emily recalled Lloyd's comment about having faith in her associates. It occurred to her that they might resent her barrage of calls. "I know you're taking good care of him," she praised Sally. "I'm just—I adore him, you know. I can't help being concerned about him."

"Well, just stop being concerned," Sally ordered. "Forget about him and enjoy yourself. There's nothing you can do for him, anyway. We're taking care of everything."

"Okay," Emily muttered.

"And stop calling us. Everything's fine here."

Sally sounded brusque to Emily, eager to end the call. Evidently she and Tom were overworked, and Emily smothered a twinge of guilt at having abandoned them for the week. "Okay, Sally," she mumbled. "I'll stop being such a pest."

"Good girl. We'll see you next Monday."

Emily asked Sally to give her regards to Tom, then said good-bye. She joined Lloyd outside the booth. "What did Tom say?" he asked.

"I talked to Sally—Tom was busy spaying somebody." Emily offered a sheepish smile. "Sally told me to stop badgering them. You're right, Lloyd. I should have faith in them."

Lloyd measured her with his gaze. "What did she say about Gus?" he asked.

"She said they knew what to do for him. I'm sorry I've been so frantic, Lloyd." She gave him an impulsive hug. "I won't call them anymore. Everybody wants me to relax, so I might as well do that. I seem to be outnumbered three to one."

Lloyd returned her hug and touched his lips to hers.

"Let's get some food," he said as he ushered her into the supermarket.

Once they'd stocked up on groceries, they returned to the cabin to drop off their purchases. They fixed peanut butter sandwiches for themselves, ate their lunch, and then drove south to the town beach. Lloyd's friend had provided them with a resident sticker for the car so they'd be allowed to use the beach.

Owing to the fact that the summer season hadn't yet started, the beach was fairly empty. Emily and Lloyd strolled along the water's edge, wading into the freezing water and then racing back to the sand. Emily thought briefly about how much Gus would enjoy romping on the beach. As soon as he was completely recovered, she'd bring him to the shore. And Lloyd, too. They'd all take a vacation together.

After several hours of exploring the beach, skipping stones into the water and gathering shells, they returned to the cabin to dress for dinner. They located an inexpensive seafood restaurant in town and gorged on steamed lobsters. Then, although it was early, they retired to the cabin.

The unheated room was cool, and they quickly undressed and snuggled into the absurdly narrow bed. They arranged themselves on their sides, Lloyd's arms looped around Emily to keep her from falling over the edge of the bed. Their heads rested close together on the small foam pillow, so close they could kiss without even moving.

They did, a long, languorous kiss that permeated Emily's flesh, infusing it with the exquisite tension she now recognized and relished. When Lloyd eased back from her, his mustache brushed silkily against her lips and she smiled.

Careful not to disturb their precarious balance on the bed, she lifted her index finger and ran it lightly over the soft black hair adorning his upper lip. "When did you grow this?" she asked.

"In college," Lloyd replied.

"Your badge of rebellion?" she teased.

"One of many such badges, I'm afraid." He closed his eyes, conjuring up a picture of himself in his youth, and chuckled. "You don't want to know how long my hair was," he warned.

"But. . ." Emily raised her hand to the thick black curls framing his face. "But it's so curly!"

Lloyd laughed again. "According to my mother, I looked like someone whose big toe was permanently stuck inside an electric socket."

Emily joined in his laughter. "What do mothers know?" she muttered. "I bet you looked gorgeous."

Lloyd mused for a moment, his fingers twirling through the ends of Emily's gently waving tresses as they spread down her back. "I looked passable, I suppose," he admitted modestly. "But I don't know that I could have held my own against a budding Hollywood star."

Her eyes sharpened, surprised and oddly flattered by the subtle jealousy that tinged his words. "Believe me, you could have more than held your own," she consoled him, then succumbed to a smile at her own memories. "Ed was pretty hirsute when I met him, too. Not exactly a polished matinee idol. If he had been, I doubt I would have given him a second look. My tastes always ran to. . . ." She groped for the right word.

"Puppy-dog types?" Lloyd supplied, his eyes glimmering with amusement.

"I guess so," Emily granted, her cheeks dimpling. "Eddie looked like a friendly mutt when we first met. I greatly preferred that to his appearance out in Los Angeles, when he suddenly became a narcissist. He was absolutely obsessed with his looks. He went to a hair stylist three times a week, slathered organic ointments all over his face, and acted like a prima donna. At first it was only because of the pressure from his show's producers that he always look perfect. But he caught the bug eventually, and took to preening until he became unbearable. Then he started in on me."

Lloyd frowned slightly. "What did he want to change about you? You're beautiful, Emily."

She shrugged. "He thought I should lose weight. He bought me this cream that was supposed to fade my freckles. He wanted me to lighten my hair. He thought I looked like a corn-fed rube—which was what I was. I don't know what he expected of me."

Lloyd measured her calm tone. "Why aren't you bitter?" he asked, intrigued. "You seem so well-adjusted."

She laughed at his choice of words, then confirmed them with a nod. "I guess I'm not the bitter type," she allowed. "I'm much happier now than I was then. Particularly right this minute," she added in a whisper.

Lloyd reflected her smile. His hands moved down her back to her bottom, and she slung her upper leg around his hips to hold herself on the bed. Lloyd's hand ran over the smooth expanse of her thigh. "I love your legs," he murmured.

Emily groaned. "They're sturdy peasant legs," she complained. "That's what Eddie used to call them."

"Sturdy, yes," Lloyd agreed, his fingers meandering across her skin, sliding to her inner thigh. "That's why I like them."

She thought briefly about his wife's useless legs, but said nothing. She couldn't speak; tension was mounting inside her, spreading up from Lloyd's fingers to her chest, seizing her heart.

He rolled onto his back, bringing her on top of him so she wouldn't fall. His lips grazed her throat before he arranged her higher on his body, affording his mouth access to her breasts. Sparks of ecstasy leaped along her nerve endings as her fingers twined compulsively through his hair, clinging to him as arousal blossomed inside her.

He tightened his hold on her and made them one. Emily had never made love this way before, dominating their motions. The sensation momentarily stunned her. His hands urged her to move, twisting her hips around him in a lazy figure eight. She shuddered as thrills of yearning trembled upward inside her.

Gradually he loosened his hold on her, and the movements were her own, her need directing her body. He slid one finger tantalizingly along the base of her spine and she shuddered once more, Lloyd's name emerging again and again from her throat in a husky moan. He arched from the bed, forging deep inside her, conquering her body with ravishing thrusts. She felt the explosive energy of their joining shear through her, consuming her, breaking over her like the ocean's thundering tide, then lapping at her in decreasing waves of bliss. Before the waves had ebbed completely Lloyd hurled himself into her throbbing heart and let the tide carry him away.

With a quiet sigh, she dropped wearily onto him, the softness of her body accommodating the unyielding bones and muscles of his. They held each other, silent, their souls washed back to solid earth where they rested in utter tranquillity.

Emily had been ordered to escape for a few days, to relax. She couldn't help but relax. The cabin was rustic, the ocean water too cold to enjoy, but spending time with Lloyd was all Emily needed to be happy. As crowded as they were in the small bed, she felt more comfortable that night than she ever felt alone in her spacious bed at her home. She put thoughts of Gus out of her mind and discovered an immeasurable content-ment in Lloyd's protective embrace.

Friday morning they found a bicycle rental shop in

town and rented two bikes. They toured the shoreline roads, avoiding the heavily traveled main routes. Emily was saddened to think that, like boating, playing tennis, and mending porches, biking was another delightful activity Lloyd hadn't been able to share with his wife. But Emily's sadness was overtaken by the pleasure of knowing that he could enjoy such activities with her now.

She remembered what Lloyd had said the night he'd told her about his wife: that love meant doing things together, working and playing, arguing and sex. She was glad she'd bought Lloyd the plants for his apartment, even if his initial response had been to fight with her about them. She enjoyed arguing with him as much as biking with him, strolling on the beach with him, making love with him. To Lloyd, those things were the very substance of love.

She risked glancing away from the road to observe him on his bicycle beside her and their gazes met. Emily saw the love she felt for him mirrored in the crystal-blue depths of his eyes.

On Saturday they decided to drive to the tip of the Cape. They explored Provincetown, the village that occupied the very end of Cape Cod. It was cluttered with overpriced shops and boutiques, its streets jammed with flamboyant tourists. Emily clung to Lloyd's hand as they wandered around looking at the people and shops.

It seemed slightly crazy that she could find herself so in love with Lloyd in such a relatively brief time. Yet it was true. At the beginning of their relationship she might have argued that her love was based only on Lloyd's ability to awaken her passion and satisfy it. But even at the start, she knew sexual satisfaction wasn't what made her love him. She'd recognized that she was in love with him even before they'd made love the first time. She had discovered her love for him when he'd

167

opened up to her, when she'd found the marvelous soul lurking beneath his defensive shell. It was his soul she loved, at least as much as his body. It was his kindness, his generosity, his willingness to open up more and more to her. Her love flourished from the trust that bound them together.

Even before Ed had actually cheated on Emily, she'd never trusted him as completely as she now trusted Lloyd. With good reason—she hadn't trusted him in bed. And she hadn't trusted him emotionally, either. He'd claimed that he loved her, yet he was always demanding that she change, lose weight, bleach her hair to a lighter, more glamorous shade. When he confessed things to her, his confessions were meaningless; he'd as soon open his soul to a stranger at the tennis club's bar as to Emily. His confessions stemmed not from trust but from his efforts to prove that trust, as Emily defined it, was an unnecessary emotion, something old-fashioned and puritanical.

But Lloyd understood the real meaning of trust. It was something he valued as highly as Emily did. That was why she loved him.

They left Provincetown in the afternoon and drove back to Dennis Port. Lloyd chose an elegant resort in the next town for their last dinner on the Cape; his friend Glenn had recommended the place. Emily readily agreed that they should celebrate.

After Emily showered, she put on the fanciest dress she'd brought with her. Of muted turquoise linen, it had a low-cut neckline and blousy sleeves. It hugged her body's voluptuous curves in a way that used to make her self-conscious. But Lloyd liked her figure, and she suspected he'd appreciate the way the dress displayed her hourglass shape.

He did. When she emerged from the bedroom to join him in the living room, his eyes absorbed her and his lips spread in a seductive smile. He crossed the small room in two long strides and bent to kiss her throat. "I'm tempted to suggest that we skip dinner," he murmured.

"Isn't that my line?" Emily laughed, her breath quickening as Lloyd's hands encircled her waist.

"Well, we know we can't get room service in this dive," Lloyd chuckled.

"Look, mister," she teased, "if you're thinking what I'm thinking, we probably should get some food into our systems first. We'll need it to keep up our energy level tonight."

"You, Emily Squires, have a very naughty mind," Lloyd clucked indignantly as he escorted her from the cabin.

Emily found it hard to keep her eyes off him as he drove down the main road to Harwich Port. He looked absolutely gorgeous in his lightweight khaki trousers, white shirt, and dark blue blazer. The few days he'd spent in the sun had burnished his naturally bronze skin, giving it an even richer glow. His eyes were as dazzlingly blue as she'd ever seen them.

The resort Lloyd's friend had recommended was nestled on the beach. The dining room overlooked the grassy dunes and the ocean beyond, and a small combo provided romantic music to accompany their meal. Emily was only vaguely conscious of the food; she was far too atuned to Lloyd's presence, and to the sublime night they would spend in each other's arms, to pay much attention to her meal.

"Let's take a walk on the beach," Lloyd suggested when they'd washed down their dinner with coffee. Emily happily agreed. Prolonging the anticipation of what would happen when they returned to the cabin would only make her enjoy it more.

They left the dining room and ambled across an

adjacent terrace to the beach. A cool breeze lifted off the water; the tide surged gently against the shore. The sun had set, but the sky was still pale, with only a few stars piercing its clear expanse. Lloyd and Emily had the beach to themselves.

Lloyd seemed oddly preoccupied as he took Emily's hand and meandered along the empty white sand with her. She wondered if he too was thinking about the night that lay before them. He seemed wistful, his lips twisted in a poignant smile. Perhaps his thoughts extended beyond the night. Tomorrow they would be returning to Hartford, and Emily would be leaving him, returning home to New Preston. But there would be other weekends. Tomorrow wouldn't mean good-bye. As Tom had pointed out, Hartford wasn't so far away.

Lloyd came to a halt several yards from the foaming water. He removed his blazer and spread it across the sand, then gestured to Emily that she should sit. Surprised, she obeyed, and he dropped onto the sand beside her. She turned expectantly to him. "There's something I want to tell you," he said solemnly.

She peered into his eyes, and a small fire ignited inside her. His earnest expression thrilled her. She instinctively knew what his eyes were saying, what he wanted to tell her. He wanted to talk about love. He hadn't yet told her in words that he loved her. She was acutely aware of how much of an effort it was for Lloyd to express his feelings verbally.

"There's something I want to tell you, too," she whispered.

He appeared bemused. "Maybe you should go first," he invited.

"I love you," she said unflinchingly.

He studied her, savoring her words, his eyes velvet soft in the waning light. "Oh, Emily," he breathed before ringing his arms around her and drawing her

170

mouth to his. His lips played over hers like a magic spell, shaping themselves to hers, blessing her tongue with potent caresses.

"Let's leave. Let's go back to the cabin," he murmured.

She struggled to regain her composure, waiting until her heartbeat slowed before she dared to speak. "You said you wanted to tell me something," she reminded him softly.

"Right." He lifted his hand from her and turned toward the water, his gaze fixed on the horizon. He was silent.

"Well?" she prodded him, every nerve in her body receptive to him, to the wonderful words she expected to hear.

He took a deep breath. "Gus is dead," he murmured.

Emily didn't move. She felt the heat fleeing her body, her organs freezing, her spine becoming rigid, immobilized by the shock of Lloyd's statement. Her vision momentarily blurred, then focused sharply on his profile, his hands curled into fists on his knees and his eyes staring resolutely at the churning tide. "What?" she choked.

"Gus is dead," he repeated slowly.

She hadn't been mistaken. She hadn't misunderstood. A strange, broken sound writhed from her throat, and she shook her head against the frenzied drumming of the pulse in her skull. "What are you talking about?" she asked in a hoarse voice.

"He took a turn for the worse. The infection spread. He was in terrible pain." Lloyd's gaze dropped to the sand at his feet. "Tom put him out of his misery."

"No," Emily moaned irrationally. "No, you're crazy."

"I'm not crazy," Lloyd insisted. "It's the truth."

She couldn't look at him. She stared at the water, the beach, the sky, frantically searching the universe for a sign that Lloyd was lying. "How do you know this?" she asked him sharply, her bewilderment transforming into anger. "What the hell do you know about it?"

"I talked to Tom Wednesday afternoon," Lloyd explained slowly. "I called him from my office after you and I had lunch. He told me Gus was suffering terribly. He thought this was the kindest thing he could do." Lloyd sighed. "He asked me to take you away for a few days, to get you far enough away that you wouldn't do something foolish like drive back to the clinic and try to stop him."

Emily's jaw dropped. Then this trip to Cape Cod hadn't been the impulsive, romantic getaway she'd thought it was. Lloyd had brought her here only to keep her from racing back to Litchfield to save her dog. He'd brought her here not because he loved her but merely to keep her from Gus.

An incoherent wail wrenched itself from her and she started to rise to her feet. Lloyd grasped her wrist and pulled her back down beside him. He gripped her shoulders and forced her around to face him. His face was shadowed with pity. "Emily, I'm sorry."

"You're sorry?!"

"It had to be done."

She was shaking with rage. There would be time to mourn for Gus later; now all she could do was despise Lloyd. "All right," she snapped furiously. "All right. You did what had to be done. You did your duty. You abducted me and kept me incommunicado so Tom could kill my dog. Now what happens? Is he going to pay you a bounty?"

"Emily, how can you say such a thing?"

"It's easy," she railed. "What am I supposed to think? Tom told you to get rid of me for a few days, and you did it. You made things convenient for him so he could kill my dog. And lucky you, you got a nice, sexy vacation with me in the bargain!"

"Emily . . ."

"I trusted you, Lloyd. I trusted you, and I trusted Tom. Now I find you lied to me, and Tom killed my dog."

"He put your dog out of his misery, Emily," Lloyd said, defending Tom. "He put an end to his suffering. That's what vets do. It's what you would have done if you'd had any objectivity about the situation."

"Like hell I would have! Gus was a fighter—he would have pulled through. I know it!" Lloyd shook his head, but Emily pressed on, driven by her scathing anger. "And you! You play-acted the happy tourist routine with me. You knew this all along and you kept it from me. I trusted you, Lloyd, and you betrayed me!"

"Emily . . . Emily, I wanted to tell you but . . ." He paused to shape his words. "You were so happy, enjoying yourself so much. I didn't want to spoil everything—"

"Well, you have. You've spoiled everything." She was more upset by Lloyd's duplicity than by her pet's death. "I thought you brought me here because you loved me."

"Emily . . ."

"But it was all a lie," she whispered bitterly. "That's what this trip was about. You dragged me off and lied to me for three days."

"I didn't—"

"You did. You kept this from me. That's the same thing as lying." A dry sob tore from her throat and she rose. "Take me home."

She stormed across the beach, her steps awkward, the heels of her shoes sinking into the pliant sand. She was already on the terrace before Lloyd caught up with her. Her frigid silence forbade him from saying anything, from even reaching out to take her hand. She

173

hugged her arms around herself and stalked to the parking lot, her lips shut tight against the tears of anguish that threatened to burst from her.

She wouldn't cry. She wouldn't let Lloyd see her fall apart. She wouldn't let him see how hurt she was, how disappointed, how tormented. She had trusted Lloyd, and he had lied to her. She would never be able to trust him again.

And while losing Gus was painful, the realization that she had been wrong to trust Lloyd was far more painful. Losing her trust in him was the most devastating blow of all.

10

At Emily's insistence, they left Dennis Port right away. She simply couldn't bear the thought of spending the night curled up with Lloyd in the cabin's enticingly narrow bed. They changed their clothing, dressing in attire more comfortable for a long drive, packed their bags, and locked up the cabin.

Neither of them spoke during the dark journey back to Hartford; they were both steeped in their own private ruminations. Emily stared blankly at the colorless stretch of highway before them and tried to unravel her knotted thoughts.

Had she overreacted to what Lloyd had done because of her sadness over Gus's death? No, she reassured herself. Her sorrow about her pet's demise was one thing; her outrage at Lloyd's deceit quite another.

He had claimed that he wanted to take her away for a few days so they could be together, just the two of them. That was a lie. He'd run off to Cape Cod with her only in order to get her out of Tom's way. The idea of a romantic getaway hadn't even originated with Lloyd, Emily realized. Tom had undoubtedly suggested it, just as he'd suggested that Lloyd invite Emily to Hartford in the first place. "Take her somewhere where you can keep her busy and far from telephones," she imagined Tom explaining to Lloyd. "She's a sucker for beaches. Kansas girl—take her to the ocean; that'll distract her." As outlandish as it seemed, Emily entertained the notion that Lloyd didn't even have a friend named Glenn, but rather that he'd called a dozen Cape Cod rental agents until he'd found one who could provide him with a cabin minus a telephone for a long weekend.

So he'd obeyed Tom and taken her away, then concealed his knowledge of her dog's fate from her for three carefree days. As if she wasn't mature enough to handle the news, as if she had to be protected from the truth!

Granted, Lloyd had acted with the best of intentions. But good intentions weren't love. Emily had seen their brief Cape Cod excursion as a sign of their love for each other, and he had seen it only as a scheme to distance her from Gus, as a plot he'd concocted in collusion with Tom to dispose of Emily for a few days.

Eventually they reached his apartment complex in Hartford. They climbed out of the BMW and hoisted their bags from the trunk. Emily started directly across the parking lot to her station wagon, but Lloyd snagged her arm and halted her. "I want to go home," she ground out.

"Emily, it's after two in the morning," he reminded her. "You haven't had any rest. You'll fall asleep at the wheel if you try to drive home now."

He was right; she was too tired to drive back to New Preston. Reluctantly, she followed him into his building and upstairs to his apartment.

Without speaking, they prepared for bed. Emily hadn't brought a nightgown with her, but she refused to expose her body to Lloyd. She stubbornly donned a T-shirt and kept her panties on when she climbed beneath the covers.

Although they were both exhausted, neither of them fell asleep. They lay motionless, side by side, gazing at the ceiling, not touching. After an eternity, Lloyd broke the silence. "Emily, I'm sorry about Gus."

"Forget about Gus," she snapped caustically. "Gus isn't the problem."

Lloyd considered her words, then ventured, "I only wanted to help."

"I don't want your kind of help," she whispered tensely. As soon as she spoke the words she knew they were the worst thing she could have said to him. She wondered how many times Lloyd's wife had expressed similar feelings during their marriage, how many times she'd rejected his attempts to help her.

Yet Emily's statement was truthful. She meant what she'd said. She didn't want Lloyd's help when it entailed dishonesty, deception, duplicity. She had trusted him and he had lied to her. She had confessed her love to him, and he had in turn confessed that he had merely been collaborating with Tom behind her back.

She felt his coldness now, his retreat from her. Saying what she'd said had clearly hurt him at least as much as his behavior had hurt her. But so what? Emily grumbled silently. So he was hurt. He didn't love her the way she loved him. He'd recover. He'd find himself a woman who didn't make such demands on him, and he'd gladly forget all about Emily.

She had no appetite for breakfast when she and Lloyd arose early Sunday morning. After wordlessly consuming a cup of coffee, she took her leave of him.

She had to force her attention to the road as she drove west to the Litchfield Hills; focusing on the light morning traffic prevented her from wallowing in her misery.

When she reached the route running from Litchfield to New Preston, she contemplated stopping at the animal hospital. But what was the point? She didn't really believe that Lloyd had invented the entire story, that she could waltz into the back room and miraculously discover Gus prancing about his cage, his leg fully healed and his eyes clear and alert. If she visited the clinic, she'd find only an empty cage, and that would depress her even more.

So she drove directly home. The emptiness of her house echoed inside her, matched by the emptiness in her soul. She lethargically unpacked, showered, and dressed in fresh clothing. She considered dragging her canoe down to the lake and paddling around, just to get herself out of the house, but she didn't have the energy. Instead, she roamed out to the backyard and stared sullenly at the useless runner leash linking the two trees. She would have to remove it, she thought vaguely. But not now. She didn't have the fortitude to do it now.

She arrived at work Monday morning before Sally and Tom and shut herself inside her office, too angry with them both to be able to exchange pleasantries with them. Fortunately, her morning's patients kept her well occupied, and she didn't have the opportunity to chat with her co-workers.

Tom finally insinuated himself into her office in the mid-afternoon, during a brief respite from work. "Emily," he murmured gently. "Can we talk?"

"About what?" she grunted churlishly.

"You know about what. I'm sorry about what happened with Gus, Emily. He was in terrible pain."

"So you did your job. Do you expect me to congratulate you?"

"I expect you to understand," Tom insisted. "I know

178

you loved him. I did what I did for his sake, Emily. He wasn't getting better. He was deteriorating. I knew you wouldn't want him to suffer unnecessarily."

"Fine." She sighed. "You did what you had to do. I'm not complaining, Tom. Thanks and all that. Now will you leave?"

He hesitated, evidently disturbed by Emily's dis-spirited mood. "Lloyd called me this morning—" he began.

"I don't want to hear about it," she told him quickly. "I'm delighted that you and he are buddies. But I don't want to hear about it."

"Emily, he did what he did because he cares for you. You have no right to take out your grief about Gus on him."

"Don't talk to me about rights," Emily cried. "He deceived me. He deliberately kept the truth from me. That's all that matters, Tom."

Tom's lips moved, but he remained silent. His gaze absorbed Emily's stony frown and he diplomatically left her office.

Lloyd telephoned her at home that evening. Emily all but hung up on him. She didn't want to talk to him; she didn't want to hear him tell her once again that he'd only meant to help. She wondered whether her resent-ment matched his wife's, whether it wounded Lloyd as severely. But how could it? she consoled herself. She wasn't disabled, as his wife had been. She wasn't utterly dependent on Lloyd. What dependency she'd felt had been the result not of a crippling disease but of love. Then again, some would argue that love was a crippling disease, she mused morosely as she fixed supper for herself.

She couldn't eat it. The salad looked repulsive to her; the smell of the grilled hamburger nauseated her. She wondered whether she'd left her appetite somewhere on Cape Cod.

Her week dragged, her attitude desolate and mournful. At home each evening, she frequently found herself talking to Gus, as she'd always conversed with him before, and then looking around and discovering herself alone. Twice she had had to catch herself before filling his food dish. Her world seemed to bear a gaping hole where Gus used to live. No, two gaping holes: one left by Gus and one left by Lloyd. They were both gone, and Emily had never felt so alone in her life.

Friday evening after work she drove home, taking some small comfort in the thought that she wouldn't have to face Tom or Sally for the next two days. Nor would she have to attend to other people's pets, working her cures on animals that responded and healed. As she had every other evening that week, she prepared her dinner, stared at it for as long as she could, and then discarded it in the trash pail.

She had to do something, she remonstrated with herself, something to shake off her dreadful mood. Perhaps she could work on the backyard some more over the weekend. It was overgrown; she could clear it out a bit. Or she could shop for new flooring for the kitchen. She couldn't look at the scuffed linoleum without remembering Lloyd on his knees, scrubbing off the traces of Gus's blood, and that was definitely a memory she could do without.

She showered and tied on her bathrobe, then trudged to the living room and searched her shelves for a book to read. No Henry James, she grumbled. No management theory. Just something light and fluffy and distracting. She selected a Dorothy Sayers mystery she'd read years ago, carried it to the couch, and slouched on the cushions, hoping to lose herself in the novel's pages.

She almost didn't hear the quiet knock on her door. She glanced up from the book uncertainly. Then she heard the knock again. Her wristwatch told her that it was after eight, and the windows had grown dark with the descending night. Muttering about who would be discourteous enough to visit her at this hour without calling first, she set the book aside and crossed to open the front door.

At first she didn't see anyone. She flicked on the porch light and glanced down to find a large carton resting on the porch at her feet. Peeking inside, she discovered a scruffy puppy scratching at the sheets of newspaper lining the bottom of the box.

She looked up again, and her eyes immediately focused on Lloyd. He was standing on the porch steps, watching her, his face almost hidden by the evening's shadows. Yet his eyes were bright, piercing the darkness, neither silver nor blue but something in between. He wore jeans and a brown shirt. His hand clasped a vertical support beam as if he was too fatigued to stand by himself.

He did look tired, Emily noticed. He looked drained. He didn't smile when his eyes met Emily's, but the metallic hardness of them reached out to her, causing a sensation of uneasiness in the pit of her stomach. Perturbed by the feeling, she lowered her gaze to the puppy.

It was small, no more than a month old, with long, floppy ears and tawny fur. Cocker spaniel, she guessed, with a few other breeds mixed in. She scooped the puppy up, one hand easily curving around its warm belly. She examined its adorable face, then turned it over to determine that it was a female.

Lloyd broke the silence. "Hello," he said, his voice hoarse and weary.

"Why did you bring her here?" Emily questioned him, unable to conceal her edginess. "Is she ill?"

"She's yours," he explained, daring to climb onto the porch.

Emily still couldn't bring herself to look at Lloyd. She

concentrated on the squirming puppy in her hands. She was about to argue that she didn't want another dog, but the darling little puppy lapped friskily at her fingers and turned its warm brown eyes on her, and the protest stuck in her throat. "Where did you get her?"

"Someone in my apartment building put a sign up in the lobby saying that her dog had had a litter and she was giving the puppies away," he told Emily. "So I picked this one out for you."

Emily pressed her lips together and carried the puppy inside. Lloyd followed, shutting the door behind himself. "I don't suppose she's trained," Emily half asked as she carried the energetic creature into her kitchen.

"No," Lloyd complained. "The carpet in one corner of my living room is no longer beige."

Emily couldn't resist a small grin. She set the puppy down, and the dog scrambled across the floor in uncoordinated steps to Gus's empty water dish. Emily lifted the dish and filled it at the sink, then set it down for the puppy, who eagerly lapped up the water. Lloyd remained standing cautiously in the doorway, apparently afraid of approaching.

Emily knelt beside the dog and ruffled its fluffy fur with her fingers. "What's her name?" she asked.

"That's up to you."

"Maggie," Emily decided instantly. "She looks like a Maggie."

"Maggie it is," Lloyd agreed.

Emily twisted her neck to peer up at him. "I thought you didn't like dogs," she remarked.

"But you do," he countered.

In the kitchen's fluorescent light, she studied the lines that marked his face, the smudges of shadow beneath his eyes, the creases embedded in his forehead. "You look horrible," she declared bluntly.

"So do you. Have you gone on a diet?" he asked disapprovingly.

"Not deliberately," she replied. The puppy lifted her head from the water dish, and Emily picked her up onto her lap. "How come you chose a female?" she asked Lloyd.

He shrugged. "She was the cutest of the bunch," he noted. "Maybe I figured a female wouldn't be as likely to run away."

"That's a patently sexist remark," Emily sniffed, though she couldn't deny that there was some truth in it.

Lloyd nodded grimly. "You're right. After all, you ran away from me."

Emily didn't respond immediately to his charge. She rose, warily avoiding eye contact with Lloyd, and carried Maggie with her to one of the chairs by the table. She carefully regulated her breathing, stroking her fingers through Maggie's downy fur to calm herself. "Lloyd," she said softly. "I didn't run away."

"What would you call it?" he questioned her. "You were so anxious to get away from me that you would have gone driving off in the dead of night if I hadn't talked some sense into you."

"I was anxious . . ." She swallowed, her hands floating down Maggie's back as the puppy curled up on Emily's lap and dozed. "I was anxious to leave, yes. Because you lied to me."

"I didn't lie to you, Emily," Lloyd gruffly defended himself. "I merely withheld the truth for a short time."

"Withheld the truth?" Emily scoffed disdainfully. "Did you come here to quarrel over semantics with me? Call it whatever you want, Lloyd—the bottom line was that you weren't honest."

He closed his mouth, his eyes brutally cold as he prowled her kitchen. He swung open the cabinet that held her liquor, yanked out the bottle of vodka, then changed his mind and replaced it on the shelf. Then he moved to the refrigerator and pulled a bottle of milk from it. He held it out to Emily, who shook her head, then filled a glass for himself. He dropped onto a chair facing her and gulped some milk. "Emily," he muttered tautly. "I did what I thought was best."

"Lying is never the best thing to do," she retorted.

"You told me . . ." He sounded anguished, his tone taut and strained. "You told me, right here at this table, you told me I'd done the right thing."

She scowled, utterly baffled. "What are you talking about?"

He took another sip of his milk, then lowered the glass, his hands wrapped tensely about it. "When I told you about my wife," he murmured. "You assured me I did the right thing."

"With your wife," Emily mumbled, still confused. "Of course you did."

"Oh, come on," he snorted bitterly. "I was as dishonest as the devil with my wife. If I was as noble and honest as you seem to want me to be, I would never have left her that evening to buy her some ice cream. If I was honest, I would have acknowledged what she was planning to do. I would have stayed with her, hidden her pills, tied her hands to the damned bed. I wouldn't have budged from her side. I would never have left her alone for an instant." He sighed raggedly. "I would have stayed with her for as long as it took until she died a natural death. That would have been the honest thing to do."

"That would have been cruel," Emily asserted.

"But it would have been honest." He exhaled slowly, lifted his glass, and then set it back on the table without drinking. His lips flexed several times before he found his voice. "I chose not to be honest. Instead I did something dishonest—I pretended she wanted ice cream. I left her so she could do what she had to do. And I tried to convince myself that it was better to be kind than to be honest."

"It was," Emily insisted. Lloyd's face was contorted with the pain of his reminiscence. She longed to reach out and touch him, but she was afraid to. So she continued to pet the dog slumbering warmly on her lap.

"And that's what I did with you," Lloyd maintained, his fingers drifting aimlessly over the surface of the glass. "If I'd told you the truth, Emily, you would have raced back to Litchfield. You would have barricaded Gus's cage with your body just to prevent Tom from putting him to sleep. You know that's what you would have done."

Emily forced herself to mirror his candor. "Maybe," she allowed hesitantly.

"You would have stood there refusing to let Tom end your dog's suffering. You would have guarded Gus, making believe he was going to get better, until after a few days of torture he would have died a natural death. I couldn't let you do that, Emily. That, too, would have been cruel."

She nodded meekly. Lloyd was right; his actions had prevented her from forcing Gus to endure an agonizing death. Perhaps if Emily had seen Gus she would have concurred with Tom's assessment and let him do what had to be done to Gus, but perhaps she wouldn't have. She hadn't been rational about Gus. As Lloyd had pointed out, doctors were wise not to treat their own loved ones.

But that didn't erase the fact that Lloyd didn't love her as she loved him. It didn't negate the fact that he had done what he did not out of love but out of some misplaced kindness. She lowered her gaze to his strong, graceful hands, wrapped around his glass, and sighed. "You did the right thing," she admitted brokenly. "But I guess . . . I guess I wanted more."

"What did you want?"

"I wanted you to love me," she whispered.

"Oh, Emily—don't you think I love you? Would I

have done what I did if I *didn't* love you? For God's sake, Emily, isn't it obvious?"

Her face lifted to his. His eyes were soft, imploring her to believe him. She felt her own eyes mist with tears. "How can you love me?" she breathed. "I demand too much of you."

"That's exactly why I do love you," Lloyd said gently. "You're the first woman I've ever met with the guts to really ask something of me." He bravely extended his hand, capturing her fingers in his. He squeezed them, imparting strength to Emily as he sought strength from her. "The last time I was in love, Emily, it was with a woman who refused to demand anything from me. I wanted to give her whatever I could, but she refused to take it. I want a woman—I *need* a woman—who keeps demanding. And even if I can't meet her demands, I want her to accept what I can give her and inspire me to try harder. Don't you understand that? I don't know if I can give you everything you want, Emily, but just knowing that you're willing to ask it of me . . . . How can I not love you?"

Her tears spilled over, rolling down her cheeks. Of course his actions had been proof of his love, but she'd been so wrapped up in her own anger that she hadn't been able to recognize that obvious fact. Perhaps he'd been overprotective, but his desire to protect Emily had only been a result of his love for her. Help, even the wrong kind of help, should never be rejected when it was offered with love.

"I accept," she whispered through her tears. "Whatever you can give me, Lloyd—I accept."

He studied her face for a long moment, letting her words sink deep inside him. Then he stood, lifted Maggie from her lap, and set the sleeping puppy on the sheets of newspaper spread across the floor in the corner of the kitchen. He returned to Emily, drew her out of her chair, and closed his arms around her. His lips touched her brow, her damp eyes, the salty rivulets staining her cheeks. "Emily," he murmured. "Promise me you'll never stop coming at me."

"Like a battering ram," she vowed. "I'll never stop."

"Will you marry me?"

She angled her face to his, a mischievous smile on her lips. "I've got bad news for you, mister," she warned him. "The God's honest truth is, I *am* a love-me-love-my-dog type. If you want to marry me, you've got to take Maggie, too."

He eyed the drowsing puppy, then turned back to Emily, his fingers weaving lovingly through her hair. "She's your dog, not mine."

"If we get married, we share everything," Emily pointed out. "That's what love is all about—sex, arguing, sharing things."

"Including housebreaking the dog?"

"You've got it."

He curled his lip in feigned annoyance. "I'll tell you what, Emily," he reluctantly conceded. "You help me take care of my plants, and I'll help you take care of your dog."

"That sounds fair," Emily quickly agreed.

His mouth fell on hers, kissing her with quiet thoroughness. "We'll keep this house, too," he said when the kiss ended. "We can work on it together."

"New Preston is a long commute for you," Emily observed doubtfully.

"We can find someplace to live between here and Hartford," he suggested. "And come to the lake on weekends. How does that sound?"

"I think I could stand it," she chuckled.

"And you'll teach me how to fix things?"

"You'd better believe it," she declared. "I'll be so demanding you'll rue the day you bought into this arrangement."

"Never," Lloyd swore. "Never in a million years."

His embrace loosened, allowing him to lift Emily into his arms. "You *have* lost weight," he mused as he carried her to the bedroom.

"A few pounds," she admitted.

"Gain them back," he ordered before placing her on the bed and sprawling out beside her. And then his body did all the talking, and words were no longer necessary.

a fabulous $50,000
diamond jewelry collection

by filling out the coupon below
and mailing it by September 30, 1985

Send entries to:

U.S.
Silhouette Diamond Sweepstakes
P.O. Box 779
Madison Square Station
New York, NY 10159

Canada
Silhouette Diamond Sweepstakes
Suite 191
238 Davenport Road
Toronto, Ontario M5R 1J6

SILHOUETTE DIAMOND SWEEPSTAKES
ENTRY FORM

☐ Mrs.　　☐ Miss　　☐ Ms　　☐ Mr.

NAME　　　　　　(please print)

ADDRESS　　　　　　　　　　　　APT. #

CITY

STATE/(PROV.)

ZIP/(POSTAL CODE)

RTD-A-1

RULES FOR SILHOUETTE DIAMOND SWEEPSTAKES

OFFICIAL RULES—NO PURCHASE NECESSARY

1. Silhouette Diamond Sweepstakes is open to Canadian (except Quebec) and United States residents 18 years or older at the time of entry. Employees and immediate families of the publishers of Silhouette, their affiliates, retailers, distributors, printers, agencies and RONALD SMILEY INC. are excluded.

2. To enter, print your name and address on the official entry form or on a 3" x 5" slip of paper. You may enter as often as you choose, but each envelope must contain only one entry. Mail entries first class in Canada to Silhouette Diamond Sweepstakes, Suite 191, 238 Davenport Road, Toronto, Ontario M5R 1J6. In the United States, mail to Silhouette Diamond Sweepstakes, P.O. Box 779, Madison Square Station, New York, NY 10159. Entries must be postmarked between February 1 and September 30, 1985. Silhouette is not responsible for lost, late or misdirected mail.

3. First Prize of diamond jewelry, consisting of a necklace, ring, bracelet and earrings will be awarded. Approximate retail value is $50,000 U.S./$62,500 Canadian. Second Prize of 100 Silhouette Home Reader Service Subscriptions will be awarded. Approximate retail value of each is $162.00 U.S./$180.00 Canadian. No substitution, duplication, cash redemption or transfer of prizes will be permitted. Odds of winning depend upon the number of valid entries received. One prize to a family or household. Income taxes, other taxes and insurance on First Prize are the sole responsibility of the winners.

4. Winners will be selected under the supervision of RONALD SMILEY INC., an independent judging organization whose decisions are final, by random drawings from valid entries postmarked by September 30, 1985, and received no later than October 7, 1985. Entry in this sweepstakes indicates your awareness of the Official Rules. Winners who are residents of Canada must answer correctly a time-related arithmetical skill-testing question to qualify. First Prize winner will be notified by certified mail and must submit an Affidavit of Compliance within 10 days of notification. Returned Affidavits or prizes that are refused or undeliverable will result in alternative names being randomly drawn. Winners may be asked for use of their name and photo at no additional compensation.

5. For a First Prize winner list, send a stamped self-addressed envelope postmarked by September 30, 1985. In Canada, mail to Silhouette Diamond Contest Winner, Suite 309, 238 Davenport Road, Toronto, Ontario M5R 1J6. In the United States, mail to Silhouette Diamond Contest Winner, P.O. Box 182, Bowling Green Station, New York, NY 10274. This offer will appear in Silhouette publications and at participating retailers. Offer void in Quebec and subject to all Federal, Provincial, State and Municipal laws and regulations and wherever prohibited or restricted by law.

READERS' COMMENTS ON SILHOUETTE DESIRES

"Thank you for Silhouette Desires. They are the best thing that has happened to the bookshelves in a long time."
—V.W.*, Knoxville, TN

"Silhouette Desires—wonderful, fantastic—the best romance around."
—H.T.*, Margate, N.J.

"As a writer as well as a reader of romantic fiction, I found DESIREs most refreshingly realistic—and definitely as magical as the love captured on their pages."
—C.M.*, Silver Lake, N.Y.

"I just wanted to let you know how very much I enjoy your Silhouette Desire books. I read other romances, and I must say your books rate up at the top of the list."
—C.N.*, Anaheim, CA

"Desires are number one. I especially enjoy the endings because they just don't leave you with a kiss or embrace; they finish the story. Thank you for giving me such reading pleasure."
—M.S.*, Sandford, FL

*names available on request

If you've enjoyed this book, mail this coupon and get 4 thrilling

Silhouette Desire®
novels FREE (a $7.80 value)

If you've enjoyed this Silhouette Desire novel, you'll love the 4 <u>FREE</u> books waiting for you! They're yours as our gift to introduce you to our home subscription service.

Get Silhouette Desire novels before they're available anywhere else.

Through our home subscription service, you can get Silhouette Desire romance novels regularly—delivered right to your door! Your books will be *shipped to you two months before they're available anywhere else*—so you'll never miss a new title. Each month we'll send you 6 new books to look over for 15 days, without obligation. If not delighted, simply return them and owe nothing. Or keep them and pay only $1.95 each. There's no charge for postage or handling. And there's no obligation to buy anything at any time. You'll also receive a subscription to the Silhouette Books Newsletter *absolutely free!*

So don't wait. To receive your four FREE books, fill out and mail the coupon below *today!*

SILHOUETTE DESIRE and colophon are registered trademarks and a service mark.

Silhouette Desire,® 120 Brighton Road, P.O. Box 5084, Clifton, N.J. 07015-5084

Yes, please send me FREE and without obligation, 4 exciting Silhouette Desire books. Unless you hear from me after I receive them, send me 6 new Silhouette Desire books to preview each month before they're available anywhere else. I understand that you will bill me just $1.95 each for a total of $11.70—with no additional shipping, handling or other hidden charges. **There is no minimum number of books that I must buy, and I can cancel anytime I wish.** The first 4 books are mine to keep, even if I never take a single additional book.

☐ Mrs. ☐ Miss ☐ Ms. ☐ Mr.

BDD2R5

Name _____ *(please print)* _____

Address _____ Apt. # _____

City _____ State _____ Zip _____
( ) _____

Area Code   Telephone Number

Signature (If under 18, parent or guardian must sign.) _____

This offer, limited to one per customer. Terms and prices subject to change. Your enrollment is subject to acceptance by Silhouette Books.

DD-R-A